MY NAME IS YOUR NAME & OTHER STORIES

Once again, short story writer Kerry Langan knocks it out of the park. Her newest collection is a kaleidoscope of beautifully rendered stories illuminating, with tremendous verisimilitude, great insight, and lyrical and precise prose, the complex nature of the female heart and mind.
Janice Eidus, author of *The Last Jewish Virgin* and *The War of the Rosens*

Kerry Langan's collection offers a lovely new literary voice and a quiet, sharp, perceptive mind. These stories are intimate, surprising and graceful, a pleasure to read.
Roxana Robinson, author of *Sparta: A Novel, Cost, A Perfect Stranger & Other Stories*

Kerry Langan's My Name is Your Name, *an impressive and readable collection, is a sort of primer on the ages of women. Her female protagonists take on issues and problems that are familiar to us, struggling with identity, finding autonomy, dealing with and fighting against expectations in a wonderfully detailed world, where desire and choice are fraught with consequence. The characters are sunk deeply into their lives, and they draw the reader with them as they balance on the risky edge of decision and hope. This suspension between the ordinary and the arrival of the unexpected permeates the collection, highlighting the darkness behind the bright scrim of daily life.*
Mary Grimm, author of *Left to Themselves* and *Stealing Time*

OTHER BOOKS FROM WISING UP PRESS

WISING UP PRESS COLLECTIVE

Only Beautiful & Other Stories
Kerry Langan

Live Your Life & Other Stories
Kerry Langan

Keys to the Kingdom: Reflections on Music and the Mind
Kathleen L. Housley

Epiphanies
Kathleen L. Housley

Last Flight Out: Living, Loving & Leaving
Phyllis A. Langton

A Hymn that Meanders
Maria Nazos

Germs of Truth
Heather Tosteson

Breathing in Portuguese, Living in English
Heather Tosteson

WISING UP ANTHOLOGIES

THE KINDNESS OF STRANGERS

SIBLINGS: Our First Macrocosm

CREATIVITY & CONSTRAINT

CONNECTED: What Remains as We All Change?

DARING TO REPAIR: What Is It, Who Does It & Why?

SHIFTING BALANCE SHEETS:
Women's Stories of Naturalized Citizenship & Cultural Attachment

COMPLEX ALLEGIANCES:
Constellations of Immigration, Citizenship & Belonging

MY NAME IS YOUR NAME
&
OTHER STORIES

MY NAME IS YOUR NAME
&
OTHER STORIES

KERRY LANGAN

Wising Up Press Collective
Wising Up Press

Wising Up Press
P.O. Box 2122
Decatur, GA 30031-2122
www.universaltable.org

Catalogue-in-Publication data is on file with the Library of Congress.
LCCN: 2017937212

Wising Up ISBN: 978-0-9826933-7-7

Dedicated with sisterly love and gratitude
to my costars in the Tinker Toy production,
"The Cathy, Kerry, and Shannon LANGAN Show,"
performed in a certain living room in a house on Lockey's Hill.

TABLE OF CONTENTS

THE CIGAR MAN   *1*

DAYBREAK   *11*

RESERVOIR   *21*

WHERE TO STAY   *33*

SISTERLY   *55*

MUTUAL   *71*

MARCASITE   *81*

DUST   *89*

BEFORE DINNER   *101*

LOCKERS   *109*

YOGA FOR YOU   *131*

EVERGREEN FARM   *147*

MY NAME IS YOUR NAME   *157*

THE CIGAR MAN

It had been a disappointing afternoon for Laura. She was too small to go on most of the rides at Hillside Amusement Park, but she kept trying. She ran to the gate of each ride with her sister, Mary, and Mary's friend, Susie Carlow, but when she stood next to the height marker, the person taking the tickets always told her she was too short. Mary, ten years old and four years older than Laura, was supposed to be watching her while their parents were having drinks with Mr. and Mrs. Carlow at the Adults Only Ride, an open air tavern in a corner of the park.

"Wait here till I'm off The Mouse Maze," Mary said, referring to one of the scariest rides in the park. Four people sat in an open wooden cart painted with orange, yellow, and green stripes. The front of the cart was shaped like the pointy head of a terrified mouse, its mouth wide open as if it were screaming. The cart rode up and down a raised slanted board, traveling so fast from side to side and stopping abruptly before each edge.

Mary said more insistently, "Wait here, okay?"

But Laura was tired of waiting; she had been waiting all day. She had been so excited to come, convinced this would be the year she'd go on the big rides, but she had yet to go on a single one. Looking down at her red sneakers, the toes covered with a heavy white rubber cap, she told Mary she would go to Kiddieland and ride the baby rides.

Mary considered for a moment and said, "Are you going to blab to Mom and Dad that I didn't stay with you?"

"No." Laura scowled at her older sister.

"Promise?"

Laura nodded. Mary changed her tone and said, "Well, it won't be so bad. If you'll really do that, I'll get you one of those big lollipops with all the colors. You can eat it on the way home."

When Laura didn't respond, Mary said, "Okay? You're not going to tell? I'll come find you in Kiddieland in a while and I'll get you a lollipop?"

"Yeah." Laura turned and started to walk away. Mary called after her, "You like the airplanes. They'll be fun."

Laura didn't answer. She folded her strip of green tickets over and over and put it in the pocket of her red shorts as she walked over the pavement littered with candy wrappers towards Kiddieland. She stopped in front of a ring toss game to tie the undone shoelace on her sneaker. Crossing the laces, she looked at the rounded rubber tip of the sneaker. Baby sneakers, Laura thought. Mary and her friends wore boys' sneakers with heavy rubber soles and shoelaces in a swirl of colors. Before school started again in the fall, Laura would insist that her mother buy her a new pair.

Kiddieland was crowded. Families clustered at the green picnic tables and mothers changed babies' diapers on the grass. Babies were crying over the competing music from different rides. Laura wrinkled her nose at the scorched scent of hot roasted peanuts. Everywhere Laura looked, girls and boys were holding their parents' hands. Suddenly, she felt independent, a big kid amongst all these little ones. She walked in long, quick strides, taking out her tickets so everyone could see she was on her own. She hoped the other children were watching her jealously as they were led or strolled around by adults.

She ran and got in line for cotton candy, ordering a large when her turn came. She loved the blanket feel of the pink fluff but then her hands and face got sticky and she tired of the too sweet strawberry taste. She was considering throwing the candy in the garbage when a large woman with a shiny black purse walked by briskly, her purse brushing against the candy and snaring a good chunk of the pink ball. Laura watched the purse move away from her, its owner oblivious to the stuck candy. Frightened the woman would notice and come back to yell at her, Laura dropped the remaining candy and ran to the nearest line. She was giving a woman her ticket before she realized she was getting on the most baby ride of all, the merry-go-round.

There was a scramble as parents lifted children on horses, and Laura realized too late that she couldn't climb onto a horse by herself. She refused to simply sit in one of the wide blue chairs painted with clown faces, usually reserved for a mother juggling a baby or a toddler. Laura wondered if she could simply run off the shiny wooden floor, would anyone stop her? when someone, a man who smelled like the cigars her father kept in the dashboard of the car, picked her up, saying, "The best horse is the one over here." In the air, Laura looked down at his boots, wrinkled black cowboy boots with shiny silver lids over the very pointy toes and behind the ankles. He set her down on what Laura thought was a rather ugly horse. She liked the white horses painted with green and yellow saddles; this horse was dark brown and had a dull gray saddle. A boy's horse, she thought, dejected.

Laura watched the cigar man walk to the outer rim of the floor thinking how much it looked like the one in the gym at school, except this floor was curved and glossy, like someone had poured syrup over the wood and it hardened that way. The cigar man pulled an iron stick slanted into the floor and the merry-go-round started to move.

For a moment, Laura felt funny as the horse moved up and down beneath her, and she clutched the pole more tightly. She got used to the motion and looked out at the park circling around her. There was a man selling yellow balloons tied to a stick, taking money from a woman bending forward because a small boy was curling his arms around her leg. Laura saw the small electronic cars behind the soda stand and decided to go on that next. At least on that ride, she would get to steer.

"You're a regular little rider, I can tell." The cigar man was back. He smiled and Laura saw his big teeth with a space between the front two. The edges of the teeth were almost rippled, like they had been trimmed with her mother's pinking shears. His hair was a little like her father's, dark and wavy with gray on the sides. Laura liked his eyes, so wide and blue, like the glass eyes on her favorite doll.

"So, you like my merry-go-round?" he asked.

She looked at the pole and nodded her head.

"What's the matter? Cat got your tongue?" Again he smiled and Laura could tell he was joking. Still facing the pole, she started to smile, but then tried not to, shaking her head no.

The man leaned against the horse, steadying himself as the ride seemed to speed up. The zipper on his black cotton jacket brushed lightly against the top of Laura's thigh as he shifted his weight with the turn of the carousal. He reached into his pocket and took out his wallet, a fat packet of frayed brown leather with slips of paper sticking from it. Opening it, he pulled out a photo and held it in front of Laura. "That's me with my real horse," he said.

She looked at the picture. The cigar man was sitting on a big horse, brown with white spots, wearing a white straw cowboy hat with a red feather tucked into the band circling the brim. He was laughing at the camera, one hand held up against his forehead in a salute.

By now, Laura felt almost a part of the horse. She let go of the pole with one of her hands, placing it on the top of her right leg as she turned to focus on the picture. "What's your horse's name?"

The cigar man responded eagerly, moving his face around so Laura was staring into his open, happy eyes. "His name? His name's Skyman because he's faster than an airplane. He's the fastest horse alive." He spit a little when he talked, hitting Laura's arm with a soft, light spray. She looked down at the picture again and imagined herself on a real horse instead of this fake one. If she were on a real horse, she'd put on a cowboy hat too, and wear her hair in two braids that would swing out beneath the hat. "He's a nice horse," she said.

The cigar man was quiet for a moment and then broke into a wide grin, like Laura had proven something about herself that he had suspected all along. "He sure is. He's a nice horse and you're a real nice little girl. Stay here." He winked at Laura, bunching up his eye into a lumpy circle ringed with lines, one side of his lip raised a bit. She wanted to wink back, but it was hard for her to close only one eye.

Laura watched him walk across the shiny floor and pull the lever. The ride slowed, Laura's horse straining to rise as she looked out at the park again and thought it looked like slow motion in a movie. Or like when you turned yourself around and around again very fast and then stopped, and everything around you was still moving, just a little.

Everywhere parents picked children up off the horses, a small boy tripping and falling as he ran off the ride. He's too little for this ride, Laura thought. The people who had been waiting in line stepped onto the wood and began putting children on the horses. Laura expected the cigar man would come back to lift her down, but he didn't. He was out front with a tall woman with curly orange hair. They both took tickets from the people waiting in line. She looked down at her leg, where his jacket zipper had brushed against her. Tiny white up-and-down-lines, like the kind her skates made on the ice, were sketched into her leg. She licked her fingers and rubbed the lines, thinking she could erase them, but they stayed.

The cigar man walked onto the wooden floor and over to the lever, leaning over it and then pulling it towards him so that the back of his jacket stretched then wrinkled. The horses began to rise up slowly and the merry-go-round started to move. Immediately, he was at her side again, telling her to hold on tight. Leaning in, he put his arm around the small of Laura's back, the zipper on his jacket again meeting her leg. Laura looked around at the other people on the ride, on only for their first time. She wanted to tell them that this was her second ride, her *free* ride because the man who owned the ride liked her.

The cigar man took out a pack of gum in a dark red wrapper. He tore open the top and unwrapped a stick, holding it just in front of Laura's mouth until she bit into the top of it and opened her mouth wide to catch the rest.

"Thank you," she said, watching him as he put his entire stick of gum in his mouth at once, his jaw moving sideways as he chewed.

"Say, you've got manners, you know that? You're a very polite little girl."

The skin on her face felt hot and Laura knew she was turning red, embarrassed but pleased. "Thank you," she said this time more quietly and sounding almost as if she would giggle. She was ready to be embarrassed by his praise again.

"Who taught you that?" He put a second piece of gum in his mouth. "Your mama teach you such nice manners?"

Laura tasted the cinnamon in the gum; it stung a little so she stopped chewing and held it on one side of her mouth. "My mother and my teacher at school," she said. She watched him nod his head at her, his soft, fluffy eyebrows lifted a bit under his forehead.

"I'm going into second grade."

He stepped away from her a bit and looked surprised, opening his mouth and blinking his eyes. "Second grade? You don't say?"

"I am," she said, eager to convince him. "I already know how to read."

His arm rose from her back to her shoulder. "Well, you are one smart little girl, no doubt about that. Where's your mama now?"

"At the restaurant. The one near the big roller coaster."

The organ music was slowing down and Laura readied herself for the slow-motion ending of the ride. She knew the cigar man wouldn't lift her off the horse and she wondered how many free rides she could have. It's like my birthday, she thought, with a happy shiver.

When the new people got on the ride this time, a man with thin brown hair and wire frame glasses lifted a girl with brown pigtails onto the horse next to Laura's, a white horse with a pink and turquoise saddle. It still bothered Laura that she wasn't on one of the pretty horses, but the cigar man had said this one was the best. Maybe it reminded him of Skyman. Leaning forward, she patted the sides of the horse's face and said, "Good horse, Skyman, good horse," loudly, so the girl next to her would hear.

Laura turned to see if the girl, who looked a little younger than herself, was watching her. Annoyed that she wasn't, she spoke to her, "When the man pulls that stick over there, the ride will start." The girl didn't answer her but turned her eyes to the lever.

But a different man, a teenager with ugly spots on his face, pulled the lever and the carousal turned. Laura turned her head right and left, then tried to look behind her. She felt a hand on her back and he was next to her.

"Looking for me? Say, what's your name?"

"Laura. Why didn't you pull the stick this time?" Now the girl next to her would think that the cigar man was just her father.

"Why, I should have *known*," he said, stretching the words out, "that such a pretty girl like you would have a pretty name like Laura."

She almost didn't care that he liked her name. She wanted to know why someone else was starting his ride. She looked at him and he saw her disappointment. "That's Roy over there," he told her, indicating the skinny boy in jeans and a white undershirt still standing near the lever. "He works for me. He's going to take over for a while so I can show you Skyman."

Laura looked at him to see if he was joking, but his face looked truthful, his eyes so expecting her delight. She tingled from her hair roots to her toes and wondered how she could ever wait to tell Mary that she was chosen over all the people on the merry-go-round to see the fastest horse in the world.

But would there be time to go before Mary came looking for her? I'll go see Skyman for just a minute, Laura thought. Maybe I'll sit on him, but just for *one* minute. Maybe the cigar man will take my picture sitting on him and I can show it to everyone.

"Where is Skyman?" Laura asked. "Is Skyman at the pony ride farm?" The farm was across the street from the park. Her family had gone there last summer and Laura had ridden on a brown horse with her father.

"You know about the pony ride farm? You really do?"

She nodded, making her eyes wide to show him his question was ridiculous. "Of course I know about the pony ride farm. I've even *been* to the pony ride farm."

This time the cigar man smiled in slow motion but didn't show his teeth. He waited a few moments before he spoke. When he did, his voice was quiet and Laura could barely hear him over the organ music. "I knew you were the smartest kid on this ride, Laura. I knew you were a regular little lady." He looked around and then walked over to Roy. Laura watched them talking and then she looked at the girl next to her again. The girl had been watching her with interest, but turned her head quickly when Laura caught her eye. *I saw you looking at me*, Laura thought, *don't pretend.*

The ride began to slow and she took her hands off the pole and waved them by her sides. I can ride no-handed, Laura thought, just like the big kids on their bicycles. But then the ride jerked, almost stopping and starting again with a tug, causing Laura to fall forward and hit her mouth on the pole. Her teeth cut into the soft, wet inside of her lip and she tasted blood. She blinked her eyes as fast as she could to keep her tears from dropping down her cheeks.

"Are you okay, honey?" someone asked. Laura looked up. It was the father of the girl on the white horse. He looked at her through his wire glasses, the lenses shaped in perfect circles. The girls looked at each other and Laura felt the water on her cheeks, a few tears already sliding over the rim of her chin.

The ride stopped altogether and the cigar man came over, taking out a red bandanna from his back pocket. "Horse throw you? Got to hold on tight, little lady. Skyman will be nicer, you'll see." He dabbed at her face and told her to give him her gum which he tossed off the ride into the air. Then he lifted her off the horse and set her on the wood. Her legs felt strange after having been on the horse for so long. She looked up at the girl on the white horse and said, "I'm going to see a *real* horse." She walked off the floor, the cigar man right behind her.

He held her hand as they walked across the pavement. They passed the caramel popcorn stand and he asked her if she wanted a bag.

"No thank you," she said, again waiting for him to be impressed with her manners.

"Well, I like it," the cigar man said, "and Skyman just loves this stuff, eats it right out of my hand."

Laura watched the lady in the yellow and white striped uniform scoop a bunch of the caramel corn into a plastic bag. "A horse who eats popcorn?" she asked, now even more excited to see Skyman. Maybe the cigar man would take a picture of her feeding the popcorn to the horse.

A man with a fuzzy voice came over the public address system. His voice whistled air and spit static out over the crowd in the park. Laura raised her hands over her ears to block the loud noise. People stopped moving to try and listen more carefully to the announcer. The cigar man leaned forward a bit with a lowered head and put his finger slowly over his lips. She uncovered her ears and listened to the fuzzy voice with everyone else.

"Will Nora Sarton please come to the information booth in the middle of the square. Nora Sarton. Come to the information booth." The announcer was talking to someone standing nearby and you could hear the undercurrent of excited voices. Again the announcer came on and repeated the message. He said something else, but his voice sounded fuzzy to Laura and she couldn't understand his words.

They started walking again and Laura could see the exit gate just past the ice cream stand.

"Say, Laura," the cigar man said, "you never told me your whole name. What's your last name?"

"Carson. I'm Laura *Marie* Carson," she explained, providing her middle name since she thought he would want to know that too.

"Pretty, pretty name. But you know what, Laura Marie, I think we better go see Skyman another time. He's awfully shy, and I should have told him first that I was bringing company."

Laura stopped walking so abruptly, she stubbed the toe of her sneaker, the rubber squeaking against the pavement. What was he saying? It was all planned, it had been his idea.

"I won't frighten Skyman," she said quickly. "I'll wait with the other horses until you tell him I'm there, and then I'll come say hi to him." She was hopeful he'd be impressed again with how smart she was.

But he just shook his head. "No, he's really shy. Skyman needs time to get used to an idea."

It was too disappointing. She wasn't going to get to see the horse after all. She wasn't going to get to sit on him or feed him popcorn or take a picture. The cut in her mouth began to throb. She recognized the feel of her face being tugged to its center, a warning she was about to cry.

"Hey, little ladies don't cry. Here, you take this. You come back and see me another time." He handed her the caramel corn and turned around. Laura watched him walk back to the merry-go-round until the sound of his boots on the pavement was too faint to hear. It's *not fair*, she thought. He *promised* me. It's wrong to break a promise, her mother always said so.

Laura turned around and walked to the entrance of Kiddieland. She sat on one of the green wooden benches and swung her legs. The wood was rough with paint peeling off, not smooth and shiny like the floor of the merry-go-round. She munched a few pieces of caramel corn and then put the bag beside her on the bench.

She heard a rushing, pounding sound. It got louder, repeated thudding, like a galloping horse, she thought, now excited. Lifting her head quickly, Laura hoped to see Skyman bounding toward her, the cigar man on top of him. He had changed his mind and brought the horse to the amusement park! Now Laura could sit on him as the cigar man led Skyman all through the park. Everyone would stop and look at the girl chosen to ride him, the special girl who got to ride a real horse!

Instead she saw her parents and Mary running towards her, calling her name. The Carlows were there too. Their faces looked strange, like the wild faces painted on the outside of the spooky fun house in the big kids' park. Her mother looked happy and sad; she was smiling but pressing her hand against her forehead as she ran forward. Mary had been crying, her face a patchwork of pink and white splotches. Only her father looked clearly happy, a huge smile on his face. Laura sat upright, satisfaction stiffening her spine so that it felt as solid as a brass pole. She watched her family continue to run towards her, and she realized it had been a good day. Maybe not as good as Christmas or a birthday, but still good.

DAYBREAK

From my spot on the floor under this desk I see all different kinds of shoes. Many of the customers are tourists who wear new moccasins that they just bought across the street at the Taos Moccasin Outlet. And a lot of wedgie sandals come in. I check to see if the toenails are painted a pretty color. Every now and then I spot a pair of high tops and I look up to see if the person is around my age, eight, and got dragged into the store with their mother. Then I go back to reading my book. My goal is to read all The Babysitter Club books this summer.

My mother has given up on making me sit in a chair. I tried to but my back got tired and I started whining about wanting to leave the shop and walk around the plaza. Three weeks ago, a girl a year older than me was kidnapped and now her picture's taped to the front door of every shop. Because of that, I can only leave the shop when I go for lunch with Mom, but she gave in about the floor. "Just make sure you stretch every now and then, Jessie, or you'll get leg cramps."

Ricki, the other sales clerk, has her lunch when we come back. That hour when she's gone is my mother's favorite. She and Ricki have this competition going. Mom always checks the receipt drawer to see how many sales Ricki's had while we've been at lunch. And then she stands in front of the jewelry display and makes sure the turquoise earrings are in the front and the earrings with pink and green stones are in the back. Ricki likes to move them around, "rotate the merchandise," she says, and it drives Mom crazy. After checking the jewelry, Mom goes to the back wall and makes sure all the framed pictures are hung in their proper place. She has them arranged in a certain way and she goes ballistic if each one isn't where it's supposed to be.

When I'm not reading, I'm staring up at the pictures. Most of them are of pretty women with long flowy hair or hair that's short and curly around their face. I've heard my mother and Ricki tell many customers that each one is "a genuine Maxfield Parrish print." In most of the pictures, there's a dreamy blue sky, so deep and pretty I want to fall into it. Even though I'm inside, I like to think that the skies in all the pictures are real, that I'm staring up at the beautiful blue blanket that covers the world. My favorite picture is "Daybreak," the one with the girl about my age lying between the enormous pillars that look so old and big. There are tiny, tight flowers hanging in bunches over the pillars and curling around them. In the background are these enormous mountains. The girl is wearing a toga that's held in place with a gold scarf that wraps around and around her. She's so happy, smiling, because her friend, a little boy, is leaning over her and letting her know it's time to get up and play. The little boy isn't wearing anything but that's okay. My little brother, Josh, and me used to take baths together before he died. And like the little boy in the picture, Josh used to come wake me up in the morning. Mom called him her "early bird" but warned him to let her sleep on days she didn't have to work. So, as soon as he got up, he'd scamper over to my bed and stare at me until I opened my eyes. Then we'd laugh. I don't know how I knew he was there, but I'd always wake up and see him standing there, smiling because he knew any second we'd start laughing.

When I look at this picture, I like to think that the little boy is Josh, that he's come to play with me. I imagine taking his hand and running off into those big mountains. Of course, in real life, we'd build something with his Legos or watch cartoons on TV. Mom says Josh is in heaven, a place so pretty we can't even imagine it. Well, I think nothing could be prettier than this Maxfield Parrish picture. It is heaven.

Sometimes Ricki catches me staring at the picture and says, "Communing with your soulmates?" She says all kinds of stuff like that, uses big words to make something easy sound hard. She clutches crystals and amethysts because she wants to "internalize their energy," and tells us our horoscopes every day. I'm Aquarius, and Ricki says water is very important to me. Maybe. The skies in the Maxfield Parrish pictures do look like pretty turquoise water. On these hot sticky days I'd love to swim in his ocean skies.

One day the newspaper told Ricki that Capricorns, her sign, have a gift for business. She couldn't wait to tell the owner of the store about that. That's Eddie Schenk. Mom and Ricki call him Mr. Ed. He's an okay guy. He comes in the shop once a day and checks things out, makes sure the jewelry is selling. He's got a couple other stores in the plaza and sometimes he brings stuff from those places to sell here. Ricki doesn't like that. "Disorganizes the inventory," she says, setting her hand on the hip of her blue jeans, pants so tight she can't slip even the tips of her fingers in the pockets. Mom, though, she's quick to take the stuff from him, puts the incense on the little table next to the leather pouches or moves the sunglasses so she can arrange the new coffee mugs.

Mr. Ed's no help when it comes to Mom and Ricki's little battles. Every day when he stops in, he puts an arm around both of them and says, "You girls are doing one heck of a job. Keep up the good work." Then he usually drops a piece of bubble gum my way.

Last week, Mr. Ed let Mom and Ricki take a day off so they could attend a business seminar called, "Women on the Way Up." A lady from Albuquerque came to teach it at one of the fancy hotels nearby. Mr. Ed thought it was funny that they wanted to go but like I said, he's pretty easy. He closed the store for a day and told them they'd better make up the profits with all the "high falutin' things" they'd learn at the seminar.

I couldn't go. It cost fifty dollars a person and Mr. Ed didn't think I needed to be on the way up, although he made a joke about getting me up off the floor. So I stayed with the woman in the apartment next door but Mom told me all about it when she got home. She was so excited that she was out of breath when she talked about *delegating, evaluating, communicating, promoting,* on and on till I wondered how she could have learned so much in a single day. Problem was Ricki learned all the same things.

I knew the next day there was going to be trouble when we got back from lunch and Ricki had left my mom a note with a long list of things to do: "Run the sweeper over the carpet; dust the pictures; arrange the incense in the coffee mugs by flavor, I mean scent. You know, sandalwood, jasmine, etc. Let me know if you have any questions."

Mom continued to stare at the note. Her mouth was open as she read it over and over. "Who the hell does she think she is?"

From under the desk, I asked, "Is she delegating?"

"Never mind." Mom opened a drawer and found a dust cloth. She ran it over the front of the pictures and the cabinet containing the jewelry as well. I had to roll out of the way while she was vacuuming. Afterwards, I heard her organizing the incense sticks, tying them into little bundles with the shoelaces dotted with smiling moons and suns.

By the time Ricki got back, Mom was lettering a sign with the store hours on it. She had colored a bright gold and red border around the edges of the paper to look like a picture frame. In the center of the board was a coyote made to look like it was howling out the store's hours. The coyote was surrounded by a circle of cactuses.

"What do you think?" she said, lifting the sign so Ricki could see it.

Ricki tilted her head and pulled her lips in her mouth. "Hmm," she said, but you couldn't tell if she liked it or not.

"We need to be more *aggressive* in reaching out to people." Mom said "aggressive" like she really understood what it meant but I didn't. "Like we learned at the seminar yesterday: 'Anything you can do to make it *easier* for the customer.'"

Leaning back, Ricki raised one foot and placed the sole of her shoe against the wall covered with Navaho rugs. Over the pages of my book, I could only see her from the knees down.

"I'm not sure," she said slowly, making us wait for her words. I watched one of her hands cup her knee as she finally said, "I'm not sure it's the image we're looking for."

"Image? What image?" Mom's words came much faster.

I peeked out from under the desk so I could see both of them. Ricki was tightening her ponytail holder so her long black braid lifted a little. "Well," she looked at the sign, "those cactuses. Don't you think they're a little cliché?"

Another word I didn't know. "Cliché?" Mom asked. "Since when?"

"You know," Ricki answered, "Cactuses, coyotes, cowboy boots, they're all so, you know, *kitschy*." She twisted her shoulders like she couldn't help herself. "They're the same things you see all over the plaza. We need to *dif-fer-en-ti-ate* ourselves."

Mom dropped the sign and it fell softly to her feet. "Ricki," she said in the same voice she used to tell me to turn off the TV and get to bed, "the *name* of the shop is *Coyote* Paradise."

She nodded. "I know. I think we should talk to Ed about that. Come up with something more . . ."

She paused and I thought of the Maxfield Parrish pictures. "Authentic," I almost shouted, happy I remembered the word, and Ricki nodded again, pointing at me. "Right, Jessie. We need something more authentic. See, Jessie gets it."

I couldn't see Mom's face but I know how she locks her teeth together when she's mad and can't do anything about it. I should have kept my mouth shut. I didn't give a hoot what the shop was called.

"Well, I have some ideas too," Mom said.

Lifting her hands before settling them back on her hips, Ricki said "Great." She took a few steps and now I could see all of her. She reached into her back pocket and pulled out her cigarettes.

"I think this should be a non-smoking store."

Ricki fished for her lighter. "Ed smokes." She didn't look at my mother now as she pushed her lips out to suck on the cigarette.

"Just last week, two people complained about the smell of smoke in the store. I'm going to talk to Ed about it."

Raising her hand with the cigarette, Ricki made a zigzag in the air. "Well, you just do that."

"And another thing," Mom said, grabbing the list Ricki had left her off the counter. "Who are you to tell me what to do?"

Ricki lifted her eyebrows, like she was surprised, and opened her mouth, a little grey cloud of smoke tumbling out. "Someone has to delegate or nothing will get done around here."

Mom walked behind the jewelry counter and opened the back of it, moving the turquoise earrings in the front row a teeny bit. "Oh? And what makes you think you're the person who gets to delegate?"

Ricki walked to the coffee cups and began to stack them into triangles, two on the bottom, one on top. "Well, face it Linda, I do have more experience than you. I'm not being mean. That's just a fact."

Mom stood up from behind the counter and rested her elbows on the glass. "Says who? Just because you worked at Pizza Hut?" She was really talking loud now and I wondered what would happen if a customer came in.

"I was assistant *manager*," Ricki said.

"Meaning what? That you didn't have to scrape sauce from the plates?"

Ricki sighed deeply, like it was all too much work to explain. "If you must know," she said, sounding put out, "I did all the scheduling and I handled the customers' comment cards."

Customer comment cards. I liked to fill them out at the bakery we went to sometimes for breakfast. On one I wrote, "You should sell cupcakes with pink frosting," and on another, "Brown is an ugly color for a waitress uniform."

Mom waved her hand in front of her face to bat away the cigarette smoke and said, "Well, we work the same hours here, so you don't have to schedule. And we don't have comment cards."

Brushing her cigarette ashes into an old paper coffee cup, Ricki said, "I know. I've been meaning to talk to Ed about that too."

"That's ridiculous," she said.

"Actually, some of the nicer stores in Santa Fe do it," Ricki said. "I think it's very *professional*." The way she said professional, her upper teeth showing when she said the "fess" part, made me think we could never live up to Ricki's standards.

"Well, I think it's bullshit!"

Ricki just stared at my mother and didn't say anything. Finally, she said, "Real professional," and walked outside to finish her cigarette.

❦   ❦   ❦

Predictably, Ed was no help at all. "Geez, if I'd known you were going to start pulling each other's hair, I never would've let you go to that damn seminar."

Both Mom and Ricki told him no, that wasn't the problem, the seminar was wonderful. It just gave them lots of ideas they wanted to talk over with him. My mother showed him the sign, and Ricki had designed some little comment cards that said, "Tell us what you think!" She said that a chic gallery in Santa Fe used those very words. They both had lots of ideas about ways to improve the store, make it look nicer, but some of their ideas knocked into each other. Like Mom thought we should hang "big beautiful tapestries with Southwestern designs in the front window," but Ricki wanted to take down the drapes that were already there to give the store "a more open look." Ricki thought we should burn incense all day but my mother said some people were allergic to it, "just like cigarette smoke," which made Ricki get huffy.

"Hold on, hold on!" Ed lifted his hand like he was stopping traffic. "I hired you two gals to sell my stuff. Not to turn the place into some fashion palace."

They talked and talked at him and, finally, he agreed to one change: a new lamp. The one we had was this old white thing that reminded me of a flying saucer. It hung so low from the ceiling that tall people had to duck to walk under it. We had to open it up once a month and clean out the yucky dead bugs. Ed told them how much they could spend but warned them it had to be something everybody could live with. "Too many chiefs, not enough Indians, right, Jessie?" he said, crouching down to give me a wink.

We put the "Be Right Back" sign my mother had made on the door and went and looked at six or seven stores just crammed with lamps. There were so many ugly lamps. There must've been people out there trying to make something nice but they ended up with something that looked strange and decided, "Okay, plug it in and that's a lamp."

The few I liked, Mom and Ricki really didn't There was a large round one with a carousal around the bottom. When you turned it on, the animals actually turned. And there was another one that looked like a large plastic upside down bowl painted with bears and balloons. Josh would've loved it. But most of the lamps were glass bubbles with buttons in the middle. My mother whispered to Ricki that they looked like breasts, and they giggled. Or the lamps were huge chandelier things that would be way too big. Some of the stand-up models were okay, one had a lacy fringe, but we had to get a ceiling lamp to light up the whole shop. It was a miracle, but Ricki and my mom ended up liking the same one, a modern looking lamp with three heavy circles of glass that were clear, but kind of greenish too, around a white tube light that hung from a thick black cord. I could tell right away that we were going to have the same kind of problem with this lamp as we did with the old one. Tall people were going to bump into it. But Mom and Rikki thought it was "unique" and "really different," so they had it packaged up and told the clerk to send the bill to Mr. Ed.

"It will really send a message," Ricki said, and my mother didn't balk at the business talk this time. Instead, she said, "Wait till the girls at Taos House see it." Taos House was right next door to the Coyote Paradise. It was Mr. Ed's newest store. It was about the same size as Coyote Paradise but the only thing it sold was huge pieces of pottery. I was only in the place once and I kept thinking it would take a really big house for the pottery to fit in it.

Mom and Ricki put the lamp up right away, agreeing that nothing should be in the window so people could see the lamp from the outside. That afternoon, a woman asked if it was for sale and my Mom said no, smiling at Ricki. Things were nice, almost like they were before the seminar when there was fewer fights. When Ricki said she was going to take a cigarette break and stepped outside the shop, I couldn't believe my eyes. The way Mom rocked back on her heels, I could tell she felt the same. It seemed like the seminar really was a good idea. When Ricki came back in, she and Mom talked about inviting the Taos House girls in to see the lamp.

I crouched back into my position on the floor and started the third Babysitter book. I was almost half-way through when a customer, a man in penny loafers the color of caramel candy, walked past me with long steps and went right to the back of the store. I had that scary, dancy feeling in my chest that something was about to happen. The air around me seemed to change, to move too fast, and then stop suddenly. I felt the same way the day Josh died. He didn't wake me up that morning and I slept in for a long time. I opened my eyes when I heard Mom yelling at me to call 911 and get an ambulance. By the time they got there, it was too late. Too late for Josh. I was crying, screaming, "I called as fast as I could!" One of the men from the ambulance kneeled down and held both of my hands. "It's not your fault, honey. He was so, so sick." I put my arms around him and cried. He picked me up and walked with me a little. I heard another man say, "Bacterial meningitis," to my mother. I didn't know what that was but it did sound like something that could kill. But how could Josh have been so sick if just the day before he woke me up like usual? He'd been tired in the afternoon, took a really long nap, but Mom said maybe he had the flu.

The man in the store jingled the coins in one of his pockets as he looked over the rows of paintings. "That one," he said, pointing at Daybreak.

No! I moaned silently, scooting out from under the table. Any picture but that one, please.

My mother headed towards the table to write up the sale. She was excited; the picture was marked $495.95 and it would be the biggest sale of the week, the month, maybe even the year. Most people just bought jewelry. I felt Mom's sandal hit my leg as she almost fell on top of me. She caught herself in time, though, throwing herself back to regain her balance. One of her arms hit the outer ring of glass around the new lamp, though, and it came down, slicing into her forehead before hitting the linoleum floor. Mom fell too, her sandals sliding out from under her as if she was on a skating rink. The glass lamp shattered slowly, pieces of it bouncing off the floor then hitting the walls. Ricki, Mom, me, and the customer looked at the shards of glass, the black cord coiled on the ground like a skinny snake.

When I saw the blood on Mom's face, such a fancy red color, I started to cry. The customer helped my mother up and gave her his handkerchief. When Ricki saw that my Mom was able to stand, she said, "What kind of professional woman brings her child to work with her?" Mom seemed too out of it to answer but her eyes followed Ricki who got the broom and dust bin. As she started sweeping the glass, she said more loudly, "I have to do everything around here!"

The man cleared his throat. "Look, Miss, you may need stitches. You should go to the emergency room."

I cried harder. I didn't want to see another ambulance.

"Do you have a car?" he asked, but then said, "Oh, you shouldn't drive. I can take you over."

"Thank you," my mother said softly. I was relieved to hear her say something.

With his hand on my mother's back, he guided her to the front of the store. He called back to Ricki, "Wrap up the picture. I'll be back for it."

I didn't know whether I was supposed to go to the emergency room or not, but I ran out after them, sliding into the back of a big silver car with cushy seats. We sat in the emergency room for a while and then a woman took my mother into a little room. She had to have eight stitches in her forehead. They gave her a shot so she wouldn't feel the needle too bad and sent her home with a little tube of greasy ointment. The cut with the stitches scared me. It looked like an insect was on my mother's forehead, the stitches like creepy little legs. I tried not to look at it.

That night my mother called Ed and told him what happened, what Ricki had said about me. She apologized about the lamp and said, "You know how it is Ed. It's just me and Jessie. Her father's not in the picture. What can I do? It wasn't her fault. The shop's just too small." She hung up and sighed and said she wondered what Ricki had told him. But the next day, it was just me and Mom in the shop. At first Mom was happy, thought Mr. Ed had fired Ricki, but then we saw her painting flowers on the windows at Taos House and she told us Mr. Ed had promoted her to "executive manager" there. Then she said, "You won't be alone long. Ed's hiring another salesclerk." My mother looked like someone slapped her, but she didn't say anything. Then Ricki said, "Oh, and call me Fredericka. I'm going by my full name now."

I helped with all the chores at Coyote Paradise. I vacuumed the carpet and rearranged all the little displays like Mom asked. I tied the incense sticks together to look like crosses, and Mom made a big sign with a picture of a coyote wearing a beautiful necklace. There was so much more room without Ricki but I still stayed down on the floor when I finished my jobs.

We didn't have too many customers over the next few days and Mom spent a lot of time at the window watching to see if anyone went into Taos House. She tapped her fingers on the glass and said, "Oh, I wish our store was more visible from the parking lot."

We stayed late because Mom kept adding up the receipts over and over. She worried that she gave too much change to a customer. I saw her take a five dollar bill from her purse and add it to the bag of money she'd be turning over to Mr. Ed. When she realized I was watching her, she pointed her finger at me and warned, "Don't you say anything, Jessie."

"I won't." I was hurt that she thought I would.

"Hmm." Mom looked up at the old lamp, she had re-hung it this morning, and said in a pointy voice, "I don't want to hear you say 'authentic' ever again. What do you know about authentic?"

I laid back on the cool linoleum, my arm sliding beneath my head as a cushion. I missed the Maxfield Parrish picture, the happy girl smiling up at her playmate as the sun was rising through the beautiful pillars.

Josh can't come back. I know that. There is no happily ever after in the real world. But if I close my eyes, I can pretend that the sun is coming up and my little brother is running into my room. I can hear the sound his fat little feet make as he scampers in, and his giggles. He's so excited. When I open my eyes, he'll be there, looking down at me. I'll smile up at him and say, "Okay, okay. I'm getting up. Let's go play." Each daybreak is another chance to play make-believe. It's not enough but it's so much better than nothing.

RESERVOIR

It's the summer before I start college and I walk miles every day. "Where do you go, Lynn?" my mother asks. Nowhere, everywhere. I just keep walking. Sometimes I walk the perimeter of town and sometimes I walk up and down the streets. I might start with a north-south pattern and after a few hours switch to east-west. I know every house in Banfield, the cars in the driveways, the mailboxes, the dogs. I look at everything but I never slow down. One foot in front of the other, on and on until it's time to go home for dinner. After eating, I sit on the couch and watch television until I know I can fall asleep.

I wear black leather boots that reach mid-calf under my jeans. The summer heat is miserable, my feet roast, but I wear these boots every day. I take them off just before I go to bed at night and put them where I can reach them immediately when I wake. My mother complains that they smell, asks me how I can stand such nasty foot odor, but I just shrug. The soles have a lot of wear left and that's all that matters.

My best friend, Carolanne, doesn't know what to make of me. We've spent every previous summer swimming at the reservoir and playing tennis. For high school graduation, she got her father's old Mustang convertible. We could be cruising Main Street, wearing shades and pretending to be small town celebrities. But all I want to do is walk.

The reservoir has an airy green smell. It's the green scent of summer, of chlorophyll, of rampant photosynthesis. The sun loses its way trying to penetrate the dense leaves of the trees that ring the water. And the water itself is dark and thick and green, absorbing the sweat and energy of the swimmers.

Last summer, Carolanne and I headed for the reservoir every day after lunch. The water was warm but still felt fresh. We started by swimming laps but eventually just floated on our backs or treaded water. Our friends from high school were there and we talked in the water just like we talked around the lunch table in the cafeteria. The guys were always trying to outdo each others' dives, to see who could make the biggest splash. Hank Attelby's chest and face were always tinged red from his colossal belly flops. When he landed near us, spraying our faces, I called out, "Give it a rest!"

Hank's cousin, Billy Lockwood, was visiting from Tulsa. There were rumors that his father had died in a freak accident at an oil refinery and that Billy was more than his mother could handle. Grief-stricken, she sent her son to live with her sister's family while she raised Billy's two younger sisters. Hank bragged that his cousin had spent a night in jail when he was only fourteen for hot-wiring a car and joy-riding all over Tulsa. He'd been suspended from school three times before his mother threw up her hands and packed his bags. But Hank exaggerated; I didn't know what to believe.

Billy dated someone new every week. It caused a lot of quarrels among the girls. Friends fought over him and got in a snit whenever he showed up at the reservoir with a different girl, sometimes one who was younger than us and hardly deserving. As we treaded water, we gossiped about how insipid the girl was, what questionable taste Billy had. Mary Ellen Beamen said she'd heard that he only wanted one thing, and that when he didn't get it, he moved on and tried his luck with someone else. My friends judged him harshly, but I never bad-mouthed him. I was a virgin, but I thought I understood Billy because of my secret.

My secret. Something I'd never reveal to anyone. While in the reservoir, with my arms stretched on either side of me, I pedaled in the water as if riding a bike. The movement caused a yearning between my legs that I learned to answer. The expression on my face didn't give me away. I kept up the conversation with Carolanne and our friends, no one privy to the excitement occurring beneath the opaque water. Over and over I pedaled, my wet thighs rubbing together until I was throbbing with release. If that's how Billy felt, if his body asked a question that had to be answered, I understood.

Throughout high school, my dark blonde hair hung in heavy waves to my shoulders. Usually I tied it back in a ponytail. But today, while out on one of my endless walks, I stop at the barber shop and ask him to cut it off.

"How much, Sweetheart?"

"All of it."

I see his reflection in the mirror, the way he spikes his eyebrows and creases his lips. "You want me to take it *all* off?"

"Yes. Cut it all off. I want it as short as yours."

For a half hour I sit perfectly still as the barber snips locks of hair that fall silently to the floor in a heap. When he starts to remove the smock, I say, "NO!" my voice so forceful he cups his ears. "Take it *all* off. I want it this long," I say, indicating about a half-inch between my thumb and forefinger. When the barber finally finishes, I can't believe how ugly I look, how misshapen my head seems, how large and protruding my ears are. "Thank you," I say simply as I step down from the chair, "I'll be back for a trim in a couple weeks."

❀   ❀   ❀

I've known Hank Attelby since the third grade when he transferred from public school to St. John the Baptist Elementary. He's been our paper boy since junior high. I always suspected he had a crush on me by the way he blushed whenever we spoke. He was in the middle crowd, not popular but not an outcast. There just wasn't anything special about him. Until his cousin arrived.

Every girl had her eye on Billy. Yes, he was new and that made him special, but he also had black hair and wild blue eyes and an easy, offhand manner. His popularity with the girls earned him grudging respect among the guys. Hank rode Billy's coattails and was suddenly one of us. Unless you live in a small town, you just can't understand how rare it is that someone, anyone, gets a shot at being something different than he's been all along. The transition was too fast; we expected Hank to be more humble about his rise in status, but he acted like he'd been one from the start. He dated Billy's cast-offs and started going steady with Susie Maxwell, a majorette in the marching band. When he saw me at the reservoir, he hollered out my last name, "*Dundee!*" like we were on equal footing. But he was the same old Hank as far as I was concerned.

I was in my backyard, stretched out stomach down on a lawn chair reading a book one afternoon when he snuck up behind me and untied the back of my bikini top. As I jerked my head around, I saw the self-satisfied smirk on his face. He had rolled up our newspaper into a cylinder, and then he smacked my behind with it.

"Catching some rays, Lynn?"

Lying on my stomach, I was having a hard time re-tying the back of my suit. I couldn't get up for fear he'd glimpse my breasts. My clumsy position frustrated me. "Get lost," I said, pretending to go back to my reading.

I must have stunned him because he paused before saying, "What's with you? Can't take a little joke?"

"Ha, ha," I said dryly. "You can leave now, paper boy."

I heard him sigh and start to leave. He turned back, though, and said, "You're not as cool as you think."

Slowly, I turned my head to look at him. I let my eyes run down and up his body, a cool appraisal, and said, "Yeah? And where would you be without Billy?"

He did leave then. I heard the large wheels of his heavy newspaper wagon grinding down our gravel driveway.

❧   ❧   ❧

After I got my hair cut short, I began to eat. At first I would take a break while walking and stop for a milkshake, but now I'm carrying a backpack filled with candy bars and Oreos. While eating dinner with my family, I eat slowly, filling up my plate again and again. I'm always the last to leave the table. My little brother protests it's so I won't have to do the dishes and he will. At first my mother is flattered. I have never praised her cooking before, and she desperately wanted me to put on some weight. But now the pounds are adding up, and she's making comments like, "College fellas don't like a girl who's on the chunky side," and, as I gain even more weight, "Lynn, if you don't stop eating like this, you're going to look like the side of a barn!"

"Leave her be," my father interrupts. He says so little, this surprised us all, and even I have to stop chewing for a moment to glance at him. He's dipping his bread in gravy, his face turned downward. Her lips tight, my mother takes her dish to the sink and drops it. The ringing sound of the stoneware plate against the porcelain sink vibrates for several moments. She opens the kitchen door and sits on the stoop, the smell of resentful cigarette smoke reaching us within moments.

Later that night, my mother walks into my room and shuts the door. Leaning against it, she pulls her lips into her mouth. I'm sitting on the bed about to pull my boots off. When she doesn't say anything, I look at her and say, "What?"

She rolls her head against the door and looks at the ceiling. "Tell me," she whispers, "just tell me. Are you one of those...*lesbians*?"

I didn't think my mother even knew the word, and I burst out laughing. Immediately relieved, she laughs too, glad to think that I find her question absurd. I don't know when it happens, but I realize I'm not laughing any more. I'm crying , mountainous sobs trapped in my throat.

"What is it Lynn, what is it?" she asks, frightened. She walks towards me and sits next to me on the bed. "What is going on with you? Your hair and all this eating? Walking all over town like some kind of gypsy? Just what's going on?"

The skin on my face is slick with moisture. I run my fingers over my cheeks and slip them in my mouth, the taste of the salt biting my tongue. I wish I could eat my sobs.

"Is there something you're not telling me? What's *wrong* with you?"

Her last question slays me and my cries become silent, air rushing from me in heaving breaths.

Mother persists: "Lynn! People are talking!" She pulls my fingers from my mouth and examines them with puzzled disgust.

I lie down on my bed, turning on my side so I don't have to look at her. Finally I manage to say, "I'm tired. I want to go to sleep."

❀   ❀   ❀

Billy Lockwood had beautiful form. His running dives into the reservoir were fast and graceful. There was a moment when he flew above the water, his arms fanned like the wings of a condor, before he tilted forward and brought his hands over his head. Whenever he dived, the whole reservoir became quiet. After he splashed beneath the surface, we went back to treading water and talking. And I moved my thighs together again, the water slipping like silk against my skin.

When Billy grabbed my foot under the water one day, I panicked. I wondered if he had discovered my secret, if he was going to tell everyone. But then he bobbed up and said, "Race you across. Last one there's a rotten egg!"

It was the most attention he'd paid to me and I took off swimming after him. He got to the other side way before me but he stood on the bank and offered me his hand. "You're cute for a rotten egg," he said. We sat on the bank the rest of the afternoon and talked. Carolanne kept shooting me glances that I ignored. You could hear a buzzing of voices as everyone at the reservoir sized up me and Billy, wondering what to make of us.

It was flattering having his total attention. His buddies kept trying to interrupt our conversation, but he'd just nod at them and say, "Later." When he asked me to go to the drive-in movie with him that night, I told him he could pick me up at seven.

He was driving Hank's father's old car, a rusted Chevy station wagon that had one of the back doors tied shut. But the front seat was roomy and at the drive-in he slid over next to me and slipped his arm around my shoulders.

"You're the prettiest girl in Banfield," he whispered.

I rolled my eyes. "You'll have to do better than that."

He blinked slowly, popping his eyes comically, and I guessed that most girls just ate up everything he said. "Okay, how's this? The only reason I didn't ask you out when I first hit town was Hank told me he had his eye on you."

"That's better." I pressed my shoulders into the upholstery. "But he and Susie seem pretty cozy these days."

"Yeah, he and Susie-Q are quite the couple." He reached around into the back seat and set a six-pack of Rolling Rock onto the seat beside him. The previews started to come on the drive-in screen and noise blared in the speaker we had positioned in the window. I turned the volume down until almost all the static was gone.

"You've got quite a reputation," I said.

"Who, me?"

I gave him a smart-aleck look and he chuckled. "Yeah? What're they saying?" He handed me an open bottle of beer.

"Oh, that you're quite the ladies' man."

"I can't help that." He clinked my bottle with his. "Cheers."

"And that you drop girls like a hot potato if they don't sleep with you."

He pretended to choke on his beer. "Gee, Lynn, don't hold back. Tell me what they're really saying."

"I just did. What time is this movie supposed to start?" I stared straight ahead at the screen, pretending to be interested. That I'd said what I did had surprised me also, and now I had to act nonchalant.

"Well, is that what you think of me?" He stared at me until I turned my face to his. Now I clinked his bottle and said, "I don't listen to gossip," which of course wasn't true.

I don't remember what movie we saw that night, some goofy comedy. We got lots of feedback from the speaker and at one point Billy just turned it off. "It's better this way. Let's guess what they're saying." We did that for a while, pretending the actors were portraying high level espionage agents who spoke in deeply serious, staccato tones, saying things like, "My pants are so tight, I can not breathe," and "We will sell you the secrets for three packs of Rolling Rock and a goat."

Billy drank four beers and I drank two. That was enough for me to feel happy and silly, laughing too hard at his jokes. While we kissed, he kept talking like a spy, murmuring in a choppy monotone, "I think my tongue has located your ear and must infiltrate."

My secret. That night in the car I matched my hunger with his face, his body, his scent, which seemed a mixture of pizza and Ivory soap. We didn't sleep together but I knew it wouldn't be long. He knew it too and I became his girlfriend. He didn't dump me and move on to another girl because I was ready to give him what he wanted. I winced only that first time, when he entered me too fast. After that, my body moved with his until my pleasure was so enormous it overtook me, spilling out of my skin and into the night. It made me think of the summer when I was twelve and there was so much rain the reservoir overflowed and flooded the adjoining arboretum.

Carolanne and my girlfriends coyly asked, "*What* are you doing with him?" I was evasive: "Oh, going to the movies, playing miniature golf, riding our bikes." And that much was true. I had no intention of telling them that we were skinny dipping at night in the reservoir, running naked through the arboretum until we had no breath left, finally lying down to look up at the stars and twist our limbs together.

But they knew, everyone knew. All you had to do was look at me and Billy to know that our blood pulsed to the same beat, that there was this growing frenzy between us that bordered on something wild.

How long could something like that have lasted? Surely, it would have burned out, run its course with the summer. But we never got to find out. Billy's mother missed him, wanted to give him another chance. During the second week of August, he went back to Tulsa. I never even got a postcard.

In the center of my chest was a heavy emptiness. I wasn't able to draw a deep breath because of that weight lodged behind my sternum. It pressed upon me all night as I lay in bed, keeping me awake hour after hour, the clock in the living room chiming away the night.

I couldn't eat. Chewing and swallowing were too much work so I just drank liquids. When I fainted during our high school's Christmas assembly program, sliding off the wooden folding chair onto the girl next to me, the school nurse sent me home.

My mother gasped the first time she saw me in the doctor's office, my ribs straining against my skin, my limbs so narrow and weak. She had no idea that I'd been starving. For days afterwards, she would look at me and burst into tears.

During the holidays, I stayed in bed. I drank broth and started to eat scrambled eggs. By mid-January I felt a little better and went back to school. I had so much work to make up and was worried for a time that I wouldn't be able to graduate with my class. I tried to concentrate, to memorize history dates and math formulas. The distraction helped. There were still times when I had to run into the ladies room, hide in a stall and cry as softly as possible, but I was getting better. At lunch time, I sat with my friends in the cafeteria and listened more than talked. Carolanne tried to draw me into the conversation and occasionally I would even laugh. Things were improving. I could eat half a peanut butter and jelly sandwich and drink a small carton of milk.

In May, the senior class was preparing for the prom, Banfield's version of The Miss America Pageant. The hair salons put glossy pictures clipped from magazines in the windows and hung signs that said, "Come in for your free prom consultation!" Girls spent days trying on dresses at the local shops or going to fittings at some of the local seamstresses. The adults, most of whom had grown up in town themselves, had prom fever as well. Who was going with whom was discussed at the diner, at the car garage, at the public library. The newspaper did a special issue with prom pictures from the last thirty-five years. My mother has a whole prom scrapbook with black and white snapshots of her and my father standing under an arch of flowers made out of Kleenex.

I had no desire to go, but Carolanne insisted we double-date. Randy Norton, my chemistry lab partner junior year, asked me to be his date and I said okay. Carolanne had been the lead in the spring musical that year, "My Fair Lady." She had always been popular, but now she had a little entourage that followed her around school. She was a shoe-in for prom queen and every guy on the football team asked her to be his date. I was at my locker putting my books away when she told me her choice: Hank Attelby.

"*Him*?" I blurted. "You're going to the prom with *him*?"

My reaction caught her off guard. "Sure, why not him? I thought you liked Hank. I mean he's Billy's cousin . . . Oh, is that why?"

Leaning forward, I hid my head in my locker. It was starting, that tremulous feeling in my chest. I swallowed and counted to three. Slowly I realized that it wasn't Hank's relation to Billy that bothered me. No, it was something else. Hank had been nothing until Billy came to town and brought him into focus. After Billy left, my life plummeted; it was a struggle making it through the day. But Hank kept his status. Billy got him into the right crowd and he was still in. This struck me now as terribly unjust.

I emerged from my locker and said as offhandedly as I could, "I'm sorry. It's just that I've always thought of Hank as such a loser. Ever since we were kids and he cried if you said 'boo' to him."

Carolanne rolled her eyes. "That was a long time ago."

"I know. You're right." I pushed my locker shut. "But he was nobody until Billy came to town, and he was only hanging out with us because of Billy. I mean, you have your pick of guys. Why him?"

She looked at me and hesitated a few times before she shrugged and said, "I don't know. I always thought he was cute." She glanced away. "He's got that wavy hair."

Nodding, I said, "Well, if you like him, great. I'm not trying to talk you out of it."

But two days later, it was all over school that Carolanne had told Hank that she wasn't going to the prom with him after all. She hadn't handled it well, telling him that she'd forgotten she'd already accepted an invitation from Jim Sommers, a half-back on the football team.

By that time, everyone was paired up for the prom. Hank had gone from having one of the most sought after dates to not being able to find someone to go with. His status nose-dived when he asked a sophomore, a girl who wore a ridiculous amount of make-up. At the prom, Hank seemed embarrassed by his date and didn't sit with us. Among ourselves, we made plans for graduation parties that didn't include him. Occasionally, I glanced across the gym at Hank, watching him as he handed his date a glass of punch. He seemed mesmerized by Carolanne when she took her walk around the gym wearing her prom queen crown and carrying a spangly scepter. Jim Sommers, a big goofy grin on his face as he escorted her, looked like he couldn't believe his luck. Later my eyes traveled back to Hank's table but he and his date had left early.

🪷　　　🪷　　　🪷

I was tired after the round of graduation parties and spent some lazy days sunbathing in the back yard. My mother had already started her regular summer job at the public library and my brother still had two weeks of school before his vacation began. I relished being home alone. The June sun was strong in the open blue sky, the heat slipping through my skin to my bones. I was starting to feel again, to feel something other than emptiness. The heat was so relentless, so inescapably real.

But one afternoon, after waking from a brief nap on the lawn chair, I sensed my loss as if it were fresh. My eyes were still sealed with sleep, but they were starting to loosen with the moisture of my tears. I had a dreamy sense that I wasn't alone, that Billy was coming between me and the sun, a long shadow interrupting the heat. Gently, I placed my forefinger on my breast and slowly circled the nipple, desire rising in me like sweet dough.

"You slut."

My eyes opened before I realized it. Someone was blocking the sun. Hank. When our eyes met, he frowned and said, "You cheap slut."

My body lurched up in the reclining chair. "Get out of here! What do you think you're doing, sneaking up on me like that!"

He stepped forward and swung, his palm striking my face with such force I knew my cheek was stained with an imprint of his hand. Stunned, I held my face and spit at him, my saliva hitting his T-shirt. "You goddamn nobody, get out of here!" I screamed.

Looking at his shirt with disgust, he shook his head as if in disbelief. "You bitch. You fucking bitch." His voice was low and calm, too calm. The soft hairs on my arm stood, sensing menace.

I swung my feet to the side of the chair and estimated how many steps it would take to get in the house. Would I have time to slam the door and lock it? I tried to stand.

Yank! He pulled my ponytail over my head and made my face swing. "You are such a stupid shit, you know that Lynn Dundee? You are a stupid slut, that's what you are." The voice a hoarse whisper now, his mouth stretched so I noticed the points on his eye teeth. Saliva was pooling in the corners of his lips.

He was pulling my hair so tightly, my scalp ached down to my eyes. "My mother's home," I whispered. I tried to turn my head and bite his arm.

Dropping my ponytail, he laughed, "You lying whore!" With both hands on my shoulders he knocked me back on the lounge chair. He grabbed my bare feet with his hands, his nails slicing their soft undersides. I tried to kick him, but he bit down on my toes and I felt blood snaking over my feet. Shoes! my mind screamed. I need shoes to kick him away! With one jerk, he pulled me down so I was lying flat.

At first, when he was on top of me, my mind left, escaped. Nothing seemed real, even the weight of his body was a trick of some dream. The buzzing rattle of the cicadas was an odd musical accompaniment. Or maybe I was hearing a distant lawn mower. Gradually, I heard him growling into my ear, "Do you think he *loved* you? He couldn't care less about you! He called you 'THE EASY BITCH,' you know that? That's what he called you."

I thought I heard another sound, the opening and closing of a mailbox next door perhaps. Hank heard it too and jumped from me, zipping up his jeans in a single moment. Before he left the yard, he kicked my chair and said, "You say anything and I'll tell everyone I caught you touching yourself. Oh, and Billy's marrying his girlfriend in Tulsa. She's knocked up."

❦   ❦   ❦

I don't know how long it will take me to get better this time. No one knows what I'm going through and that's how I want it. All the books say time and distance can heal anything. There's nothing I can do about time; it has to pass by one day at a time, but I can put so many miles between me and Hank Attelby that someday I won't even remember his name.

I do think about Billy, but I can't let myself think too much about what Hank said. If I start, my mind gets in a loop and I feel like I'm losing my balance.

I still walk through the arboretum. It's a lusher shade of green with each passing day. There's so much brush that needs to be cleared away that parts of it are like a jungle. Sometimes I stop and sit on the little bench where Billy and I used to kiss. I take a bite of a doughnut, pleased with how it fills my mouth, how the cinnamon stings my tongue. But then the taste is gone and everything seems artificial again. I have to hurry and take another bite to remind myself that I'm still here.

WHERE TO STAY

"Where are you from?"

April Lacinak stopped looking at the road passing by them in running asphalt streaks and looked at Mrs. Miller who was angling herself around from the front passenger seat. April was getting sore from sitting on the hump in the back seat, but it seemed the polite thing to do, insist on sitting there and letting the Miller children sit on either side of her.

"I'm from Syracuse and around there. I was in Rochester for the last year."

"And you graduated from high school just this spring?"

"Yeah, in June."

Mrs. Miller nodded. "Did you see the au pair ad in the newspaper?"

"No, I saw a flyer in the laundromat with an employment agency's number on it. I called them and asked about baby-sitting jobs."

Mrs. Miller tightened the line between her lips, and April remembered that she preferred the term "au pair." In fact, April suspected that Mrs. Miller had used this French term to convince her husband they should take hired help with them to Massachusetts for their annual week's vacation. Mr. Miller fancied himself worldly although the only evidence of this April had seen was that he held his fork in his left hand. When they stopped for lunch near Albany, Mr. Miller instructed Lindsay and Lenore, his twin daughters, how to stab their French fries left-handed. "That's how they do it in Europe," he explained.

Lindsay and Lenore, Lynnie and Lenny for short, were almost seven. Although April had known the Millers for only four hours, she understood that Lynnie was the favorite child because she insisted on it. She demanded the candy she knew was in her mother's purse and told her father to change the station on the radio every few minutes. Mr. and Mrs. Miller appeared eager to oblige her, impressed with her will. Lenny looked out the window with an unfocused stare, taking a peppermint when it was offered to her. She said little, nodding or shaking her head when a question was put to her. Periodically, she opened a book of crossword puzzles and April, glancing over her arm, realized Lenny had the vocabulary of a much older child.

April had spent the last eight years, since she was ten, alternating between three aunts' households. Her mother had died of cancer when she was three, and her father had left shortly after her tenth birthday, leaving April with his older sister. There had been a few letters, then just postcards talking about a job on the West Coast, vague promises about April joining him when he was settled. When they hadn't heard from him in over six months, April's Aunt Rita worked out an arrangement with her two sisters that they rotate April amongst them a year at a time. None of her aunts said it out loud, but April understood that the arrangement would end when she graduated from high school.

Mrs. Miller opened the glove compartment and removed a glossy brochure, folded in half. "Take a look at this," she said, handing it to April.

"I want to see it," Lynnie said, already tugging at it.

"After April," Mrs. Miller said, only mildly reproving.

Opening the brochure on her lap, April looked at a picture of purplish-blue water edging a beach dotted with small, neat houses. Beneath the picture were small headlines: "What to Do," and "Where to Stay." April started to read the entries under the second headline, but Lynnie grabbed the brochure from her.

❦   ❦   ❦

The town of Pebbletoe was a small network of narrow streets crossing at right angles. Most of the cottages were solid white or a pale gray trimmed in white. There were two main streets, and one, Water Way, faced the ocean. The two tourist hotels, "The Foggy View" and "The Water Log," stood on either end of the street. April and the Millers stayed at The Water Log in two rooms; April slept on a cot in the twins' room.

Her duties were not taxing. Eating, shopping, and sightseeing were done as a group. April's biggest responsibility was to take the girls swimming in the afternoons. She helped them into their identical suits and smoothed sunscreen lotion over their skin. They spent a couple hours on the beach, playing on the sand and wading in the water. April was nervous whenever the twins went out further than their waists because she had lied to Mrs. Miller about being able to swim.

Still, these hours on the beach were her favorite time of day. April stared at the wavy water and the sky until they fused into one airy blue wall. The sun was relentless, bearing down with a blinding weight, but April never wore sunglasses. She didn't want to soften any of the bold color about her.

Several wooden piers extended into the water. The wood was old, rotting in some places to a greenish cast. Tourists walked out on the piers in clusters, in couples, or alone, all contemplating the view. April looked at their expressions of satisfaction, contentment, and smiled when the local boys who swam beneath the piers splashed water up at tourists, surprising them, making them turn and walk back to the beach.

In just a few days, she had come to resent the tourists as she sensed the year-round residents of Pebbletoe did. How silly, she thought, to travel to a town and call it things like *quaint, relaxing, away from it all*, to spend a week or two in a community and then leave it all behind.

As April walked along the streets of the town with the Millers, she felt embarrassed to be seen with them. She noticed the faces of the people working in the shops, silently bemused by the tourists with zinc oxide on their noses. The Millers bought cheap trinkets for their children, plastic fish and T-shirts that said "Pebbletoe" with the letters silk screened to look like tiny stones. Every meal was a production with Mr. Miller proclaiming loudly to April and his family that you couldn't get fresher fish anywhere. Every plate set in front of them was "the real McCoy."

April wanted to go to the locals' diner, The Rudder, and sit with the people who wouldn't leave Pebbletoe after they got a tan. She heard snippets of conversations as she walked the streets, stories about the tourist who asked for directions to the ocean and another who asked what the secret ingredient in the clam chowder was. "I told him clams," April heard the woman say. She was fascinated by how the townspeople banded together against the summer invaders, how their collective disdain of the people who came between Memorial and Labor days united them. They were a tribe. When the week was up, April told the Millers she didn't need a ride back to Rochester. She was staying.

She had to find a job. The Millers had paid April three hundred dollars for taking care of the twins for a week, enough for meals and a room at the roadside motel a mile down from town for several days while she found something. She walked up and down the two main streets of Pebbletoe considering her possibilities. A number of artisans lived in the town, people who made jewelry from polished stones and seashells. There were also potters and woodcarvers. April wondered if any of the artists needed an assistant, someone to search the beach for shells and driftwood, but each gallery appeared to be a one-person operation. She thought of applying at The Water Log, but she worried that the staff would recognize her as a former guest and turn her down immediately. She did put in an application at The Foggy View but the manager told her not to get her hopes up; plenty of people were waiting for an opening. April thought it would be wonderful to work at the The Rudder, but she couldn't get her nerve up to go in. The diner advertised their seafood specials in local print ads depicting photos of the owner, Andy Proctor, serving bowls of clam chowder to customers seated at the main counter. April knew that the customers were locals. They were dressed casually and grinning at the camera like they were in on a private joke.

That left the fudge parlors: The Fudge Bucket, Tasty Fudge, and Aunt Sally's Fudge. She tried Aunt Sally's first, but it turned out Aunt Sally was long dead and the woman who ran the shop simply said, "If you don't want to buy any fudge, I got no time for you, hon."

April told herself that she liked the look of Tasty Fudge better. It was a short, pudgy shop, as if it had eaten too much of its own product. A window ran the entire width of its front so people could look in and see the hot fudge being poured onto a large marble table to cool. Tourists stood clustered at the window watching women in their late teens and early twenties wearing uniforms the color of orange sherbet leaning over the table, turning the fudge over at its edges with spatulas, smoothing it with knives this way and that until it cooled. Inside the shop stood a hefty, two-tiered, wood and glass cabinet filled with various kinds of fudge displayed on paper doilies. A small table with a cash register stood next to the cabinet. The air was warm and sweet, a celebration of sugar, chocolate, peanut butter, rising up to the tin ceiling and pushed down again by a propeller fan that ran constantly with a whispering spin. The owner of the shop, Tom Danders, a big man in his fifties with a nose like a strawberry, seeded with heavy pores, told April she could start after Labor Day when he always lost most of his help. He told her to pick an afternoon sometime before that to come in and train.

The next day, April walked into the shop at one on the dot. Tom introduced her to Nellie and Trisha, two girls who looked about April's age or a
bit older. Nellie showed her how to work the cash register, an old steel box
with thick red buttons that had to be punched to make the drawer open. The
money part of it was easy; they sold fudge by the piece, the quarter pound, the
half-pound, the pound, and it was all the same price whether it was chocolate,
vanilla, peanut butter, penuche, divinity, whether it had nuts or not.

After selling fudge and learning how to pour it for a couple of hours,
Trisha took April into the back room, the kitchen, where it was devilishly
hot despite all three windows being open and a number of oscillating fans
whirling. A heavy woman, mid-forties or so, April guessed, stood in front
of the stove watching a large silver pot furiously boiling with foaming white
bubbles. She was big with pillows of flesh on her upper arms. Her brown hair
was pinned up with small silver clips and she wore a rolled black bandanna as
a headband. Standing with her head directly over the pot, the woman's face
was thick and red, coated with a film of moisture. Her face was pretty, April
thought, with eyes that wavered between lavender and blue, their color more
vivid because of the heat.

"SueAnne, this is April," Trisha said.

The woman didn't look up. "It's almost to the soft ball stage. Don't
bother me."

Glancing at April privately, Trisha clenched her teeth and made her eyes
bulge. Trisha put a hand on April's back and guided her further into the
kitchen. She explained that SueAnne did all the cooking and that the help
came back whenever they heard her call that a mixture was ready to be poured
on the table. Other than that, the only time they were allowed in the kitchen
was when they were washing dishes. She showed April where the soap and
rags were stored and how to nest freshly scrubbed pots. They went back out
front and Trisha whispered, "SueAnne's Tom's sister. Mess up on anything
and she'll tell on you."

April started working at the fudge shop a week sooner than she was
supposed to because Nellie went back to college early. The following week
Trisha also left to go back to school. The streets were noticeably less crowded
with tourists and the weather cooled. Every morning, April cleaned the shop,
spraying the front window although the fingerprints were fewer and fewer.
She was surprised and relieved at how easily she handled pouring and cooling
the fudge on her own. With each batch, her confidence grew. She worried

she'd be too shy with the customers but transactions were so straightforward, she soon relaxed and began smiling easily at anyone who came through the door. Tom was often absent, running around the corner to a bait shop he owned with his brother-in-law. April enjoyed being in the front of the shop by herself. She watched the dwindling tourists pass by the window and looked forward to their being gone altogether.

One morning she heard a tinny clamor in the back room. She shyly poked her head through the swinging kitchen door.

"Are you all right?" she asked timidly. SueAnne had yet to do more than grunt at her or nod her head. April saw a tumble of pots on the floor, so many they had to have been thrown there, and SueAnne was standing in front of the sink with a tilted pot, the sugary concoction moving sluggishly down the drain.

The large woman looked up, her eyes squinted in self-disgust. "Let the damn thing get too hot." She shook her head as she rinsed the pot and walked to the counter lined with bags of sugar, a bottle of corn syrup, a carton of cream and several small bottles of vanilla. "Last time this happened was twenty pounds ago."

April walked a couple steps into the kitchen. She stood, holding her upper arms, searching her mind for something to say, but she gave up and just smiled. SueAnne was scooping sugar into a large mixing bowl. "People think I'm big like this because I make fudge." She shook her head. "I've just always been big."

April nodded and then wondered if that was rude, agreeing with SueAnne about her weight.

Looking at April, a measuring cup filled with sugar poised over the bowl, SueAnne said, "From the looks of you, you don't eat nothing."

April turned her head and self-consciously touched the nape of her neck. "But I do. I eat like a horse." She laughed nervously.

SueAnne looked down at the bowl again. "Doesn't show."

April offered, "My Aunt Fiona swears she puts on weight just smelling food."

"That must be it with me." The large woman almost smiled. "Tom says you aren't going to leave and go back to school."

"School?" April asked, surprised. "No, I don't go to school."

SueAnne turned and leaned her body against the counter, denting her upper thigh. "You're just going to stay here? All year?"

Puzzled, April nodded her head. "That's right."

"Why?"

April shrugged her shoulders. "I don't know. Because I like it here, I guess."

SueAnne shook her head. "Takes all kinds, I guess." She walked to the refrigerator and took out a jug of ice water. "Tom's wife usually comes and helps out after Labor Day."

"Oh," April said, wondering if she had taken this woman's job, if SueAnne were her friend and mad about April being there.

"Not this year, though. Patty wants to sell Avon. After ten years working here, she still couldn't keep the fudge from running off the table." She shook her head. "Tom swears she don't know a nickel from a dime. He had to watch her like a hawk when she made change."

April hoped her relief didn't show on her face. "Do you like Pebbletoe?"

Shrugging her shoulders, SueAnne said, "I guess. Never been anyplace else."

"Never?"

"I went to Boston once. Didn't like it. Where are you from? Tom said, New York."

"Yeah. Western New York. Rochester, Syracuse, Batavia, I kept moving around."

SueAnne reached in a pocket of her shift and took out a pack of cigarettes, the cellophane wrapper crackling loudly. She held them out in front of her, offering one to April. April hesitated since she had only smoked a few times, but she pulled one from the package. "Thanks." She watched SueAnne lean over the gas stove to light her own cigarette and did the same, holding her ponytail away from the burner.

"Your father's job kept you moving?"

"No." April tried to exhale the smoke without coughing. She became more aware of the overpowering sweet smell of the recently cooked fudge and, as Trisha had predicted, felt slightly nauseous. "I don't know where my father is. I lived with his sisters."

"All of them?"

"One at a time. They passed me around."

Measuring a cup of cream, SueAnne asked, "Yeah? That don't sound fun. Well, I guess sometimes it's not whether you like a place, but whether the place likes you."

April sat down tentatively on the edge of a stool. She knew she shouldn't leave the front of the shop unattended for so long, but there was a bell on the door. "I lived with My Aunt Ginny for two years of high school, freshman and senior. And she just had one son. My other aunts had a bunch of daughters who weren't real thrilled about having to share a room with me."

"Cinderella, huh?"

April glanced at the floor and said, "Not that bad. But, Uncle Mel, Aunt Ginny's husband, was a jerk. He was always nagging me to join the army. He made his son join when he graduated high school." She pushed a loose strand of hair back from her face and watched as SueAnne stuck her finger in the bowl of sugar and then put it in her mouth.

"So you'd rather work here than be in the army? I guess that makes sense."

April heard the bell in the front of the store and stood, crushing the cigarette in an ashtray by the sink. "Thanks for the smoke," she said and left the kitchen.

❦   ❦   ❦

April liked her room at the boarding house on Narragansett Street. There were only four renters and the owner, Mrs. Cormer. One of the renters, Mr. Walter Toobin, was a retired theater professor who spent most of his time reading on the porch. When Mrs. Cormer introduced them, he'd looked at her, his eyebrows lifted, and said, as if reciting from a stage, "An innocent ingenue comes to Pebbletoe!" He took in the confusion on her face and stood, offering his hand. "Walter Toobin. Call me Walt. Welcome to our little corner of the world."

When they went back into the house, Mrs. Cormer whispered, "There was talk about him and a college girl who starred in some play of his. He got fired. Some school in Indiana. Or Iowa." When April didn't say anything, Mrs. Cormer said, "He pays the rent. I don't ask questions."

April's room was sunny, with windows on two sides. She owned little, just her clothes, a radio, a few books. Over the years, April had collected some furniture, souvenirs from her stays with different relatives. Aunt Ginny had given her a pine chest, and April had painted it a soft blue with a white "A" on the front. She had carted it with her each time she switched homes. And Aunt Fiona had offered a battered maple dresser that used to belong to April's father. But these were cheap pieces and April thought it would be silly to send for them, to pay moving expenses for a few pieces of wood held together with some nails. Mrs. Cormer supplied her with a small metal bed frame, a thin, worn mattress, and two cardboard chests of drawers covered with green and white flowered contact paper. "They're just loaners," she emphasized, but she took April with her to flea markets and garage sales. April bought some mismatched sheets, a night light with a base made of sea shells, and a small bookshelf that she painted white. At a church re-sale, she bought an old picture of President Kennedy and hung it on the wall of her room. She'd noticed that lots of shops in Pebbletoe had frayed and peeling pictures of him in cheap frames.

At night, April lay on her bed and felt the wind from the open windows flow over her body. The gusts carried the biting smell of salt. She inhaled deeply and felt the ocean air strengthening her.

She came to think of herself as the main employee at the fudge parlor. Of course, SueAnne made all the fudge and Tom was the manager, of sorts, but she was the person who dealt with the customers. Tom realized he had made a good choice in hiring April, and was out of the shop most of the day now. In addition to the bait shop, he also owned part of a boat rental business. April realized that many people in town had a couple jobs. SueAnne did janitorial work some evenings at a church, and waitresses did laundry for the hotels. April didn't look for a second job because she made enough money at the fudge shop to pay her rent and buy food, and she was happy with that. At the end of her first month, Tom gave her a five dollar a week raise. Although pleased with the bigger paycheck, April was happier with Tom's confirming her sense that he couldn't run the place without her.

Eventually, she got to know most of the "Pebbles," as the townspeople referred to themselves. People gave fudge as gifts, bought it for parties, bridge games, bingo games, and church suppers. Business was a third of what it was in the summer, but the townspeople came in and April stayed busy. She shopped for supplies, putting the "Be Right Back" sign on the door as she ran to the market, and she kept a careful business ledger. She wrote the ads that appeared in the weekly "Pebbletoe Shopper" and convinced Tom to run a special on a different flavor of fudge each week. April also suggested that they try a delivery service to the hospital in the next town. Tom drove his old station wagon there a couple times a week and April told him to leave flyers at the nurses' stations. The other two fudge parlors followed suit so April suggested offering a ten percent discount on Tuesdays and Thursdays. Even if the other shops copied that, Tasty's was still doing more business than it ever had in autumn, and Tom was happy. He gave April a second small raise but asked her not to mention it to SueAnne. April said, "Oh, if it's going to cause a problem, you don't have to, Tom," but he waved his hand and said, "No, you earned it, but none of the temporary help has ever gotten two raises."

April met his eye and said, "But I'm not temporary."

Nodding quickly to make up for his error, Tom said, "That's right. You're a real employee now so you get a second raise. But mum's the word." He put his finger to his lips.

Many of the residents of Pebbletoe were intrigued with April. "You came here for a visit and decided to stay?" they asked her over and over. "A young girl like you?" Older women smiled at her as she walked down the streets and all the shopkeepers called hello to her. April sensed them thinking, *she chose us*, and felt the residents choosing her in return. A couple of the young mothers were especially friendly and she walked with them and their children on the beach. They introduced her to their brothers and brothers-in law, and April went out on dates with them. Pebbles married young but she didn't want to get serious with anyone.

She bought a second-hand bike and on Sundays, her day off, rode for miles along the ocean towns. Her muscles ached for a time but then her calves became muscular and her face tanned so dark, she looked as if she worked on one of the boats. Every now and then, someone mentioned that she didn't sound like she was from the area but, other than that, April knew she fit in with the locals.

Mrs. Cormer ran the bingo games played in the town hall on Monday nights, and April went with her out of politeness, happy to help with the coffee urns and lose a few dollars to stay on Mrs. Cormer's good side. One week, two women argued loudly after one spilled coffee on the other's card and the other accused her of having done it on purpose. Mrs. Cormer shouted, "Keep it up and you'll both be suspended for a month!" Later when gathering up the used Styrofoam cups for the trash, an older woman who'd won early in the night winked at April and said, "Your landlady runs this bingo parlor like cell block nine." April lifted her eyebrows and realized that she'd worried so much about how the locals felt about her that she'd never bothered to consider how they felt about each other. When the tourists were there, they'd seemed like one big happy family. For the first time, April realized that the town needed the tourists, and not just for money.

❧ ❧ ❧

Each morning when she walked into the kitchen, SueAnne looked up from the stove and said, "Still here, huh?" April tried to get to know SueAnne, asking her if she wanted to have dinner with her at The Rudder, but she always had plans. SueAnne was popular with a certain group of women, women who worked at the bowling alley and the arcade. This group had been slower to acknowledge April. Only a few of them regularly spoke to her. On their breaks, the women often dropped by the shop, smoking with SueAnne in the kitchen. Sometimes April would go back to get a pot of fudge and the kitchen was filled with columns of blue-white cigarette smoke, the smell of nicotine fighting with the sugary aroma. April wondered if Tom cared about all the traffic in the kitchen, or that SueAnne's friends often sampled the fudge.

"Bring me a piece of that peanut butter after it cools," Kaye Shimmick would call after April as she carried a pot of fudge to pour out in the front room. "Me too," a few others would say. When the fudge was ready, April would cut several small pieces and carry them to the back room on wax paper. Once, SueAnne's friend Alice Ransale held up a piece of chocolate fudge between her fingers and said, "Pretty chintzy piece." April, uncertain what to say, looked at SueAnne who told her, "Bring a few more pieces back."

"And cut them *big*, Pixie Stick," Alice said. "Otherwise, I might have to take my business elsewhere." She laughed, the other women joining in. Kaye said, "She is a pixie stick. Look at the size of her."

In the front of the shop, April stood over the marble table, her face flushing with anger, and sliced the fudge into pieces as big as brownies.

❧ ❧ ❧

Tom called her before she left for work one morning in early April. "SueAnne's sick," he said; "The doctor says she might have to get her gall bladder out."

"Oh, no."

"Yeah, it bothers her on and off but she ate barbecue last night and it about killed her."

"Can I do anything?"

"No. But we're going to have to close the shop."

"Close?"

"Yeah. I won't be able to pay you for the days we're closed. I'm sorry. If she gets to feeling better, we'll open."

April swallowed and blurted, "Tom, I can make the fudge."

"What's that?"

"I can make the fudge. I've watched plenty of times. We've got so many orders for Mother's Day, we don't want people going to Aunt Sally's or The Parlor."

Tom was silent a few moments. April listened to his breath rasping into the receiver and imagined the absent look on his face.

"Well, I guess that would be okay," he said. "If it's just for a few days and we've got orders. You're sure you know how to do it?"

"Positive. I could make it in my sleep." When he didn't respond, April shut her eyes tightly, inhaled, and tried to sound nonchalant as she said, "Oh, before I forget, the bank called yesterday." Tom often carried his mail into the shop. April had seen the overdraft notices. The boat rental business was always in trouble and the bank called the shop looking for Tom almost every week. They hadn't called yesterday but Tom would never doubt that they had. "I told them you were out but I'd give you the message." She opened her eyes and waited.

Tom cleared his throat. "Yeah, I'll get back to them. Well, okay. We can't miss Mother's Day. That wouldn't be right. SueAnne will understand that."

Her breath pouring out of her, April bent over and said, "Of course she will."

April had never made fudge in her life but she knew she could do it. She had spotted a candy thermometer in Mrs. Cormer's kitchen but when she asked to borrow it, Mrs. Cormer became enthused and sang out, "I used to make fudge! Let's make some together."

It was fun being in the kitchen of the lodging house with Mrs. Cormer. She told April, "Call me Helen," and April said, "That was my grandmother's name!" She only had a single memory of the woman who took her to buy new shoes when she was three. A woman with a shiny black purse who had told April not to press so hard on the heels of little brown shoes that buckled on the sides.

"Like this," Helen said, plunging the thermometer into the foaming pot. "Yup, two-hundred and thirty-five degrees, she's ready to go."

April's first batch at the shop was a little sweet, but it was fudge after all, she told herself. It was easy, the same basic recipe over and over with just a few substitutions depending on the flavor. By the third day, April was taking chances, adding the juice of a couple oranges to the chocolate fudge, and using almond paste to invent a fudge. A week went by. SueAnne went into the hospital for surgery. April made a large card for her out of poster board as well as a bouquet of flowers made out of construction paper. SueAnne was asleep when April went to the hospital but she positioned the card so SueAnne could see it as soon as she woke up. "Get Better! I Miss You! Love, April." She'd hesitated about writing "love," but that's how people signed cards, wasn't it?

Then a second and a third week went by, SueAnne at home recuperating and under doctor's orders to lose weight. Tom said she was having a hard time, that she didn't want to see anyone. April felt bad for her but it was wonderful not having Kaye and Alice and the others in the shop.

Orders from the hospital increased but that was nothing compared to a tiny blurb in a Boston magazine about the "unexpected treat of artisanal fudge at Tasty Fudge, the standout amongst the fudge parlors of Pebbletoe." Helen proudly taped the clipping to her refrigerator, hugging April tightly as she exclaimed, "And *who* taught you to make fudge, young lady!"

Walter Toobin chuckled and said to April, "How very all-about-Eve of you."

"What?"

He waved his hand. "Nothing, nothing." His voice deepened as he extended his arm and announced, "Young April, the mover and shaker of our little community. Why, she's going to put Pebbletoe on the map!"

Helen waved him off and said, "Oh, you, always playing a part. Stop talking and get down there and buy some fudge."

"Oh, I shall!" He winked at April. "We'll be saying, 'We knew you when.'"

April smiled. That expression she knew, and despite Walter's silly acting, she understood that she had accomplished something.

The time was right to ask Tom to consider selling things other than fudge. "We could branch out, sell muffins and cookies, put a couple tables over by the wall so people could sit down and eat, drink some coffee."

She expected he'd object, that he'd say something about stepping on the diner's toes. Andy, The Rudder's owner, was one of Tom's fishing buddies, but Tom was so buoyed by the success of the gourmet fudge, he was willing to at least listen. "Well, I'll have to talk to SueAnne and see if she'll make the other stuff. But it's gonna be a while before she's back on her feet."

"I can bake the muffins," April interrupted. "I can come in early and get a couple batches done before SueAnne even starts on the fudge." April had come to relish her time alone in the kitchen. The still cool morning air breezing through the windows, her first cup of coffee as she was starting the fudge. She'd miss that when SueAnne came back. She wouldn't mind coming in at dawn if it meant she could have the kitchen to herself for an hour and a half. SueAnne wouldn't let her help with the fudge, ever, April knew that. But if the kitchen was in order and she was already out front when SueAnne arrived, she couldn't object. April thought about a shelf in the cabinet with a little sign, "April's Muffins." One little shelf. All her own. The muffins would sit on paper doilies, pretty doilies that *Pebbletoe This 'N That* sold in pastel shades of pink, blue, and yellow.

"Maybe," Tom said, but she could tell he was reluctant.

"I could make them twice as big as The Rudder's. But we wouldn't charge more. I've added up the cost. We'll still make a profit."

Tom lifted his cap and inhaled. "Golly, April. Where'd you come from?"

April blinked. "Who cares? I'm here now."

The next day, April came in the shop at six o'clock. Helen had lent her a few cookbooks and April had marked the pages with two recipes for muffins, applesauce and cranberry, as well as a recipe for cinnamon cookies. At nine-o'clock, when Tom walked in, the display cabinet was filled with the baked goods, and April had placed a handwritten sign in the window, "Special Today: Fresh Muffins."

Tom stood in front of the cabinet, scratching his head. "SueAnne wasn't too happy 'bout the idea," he told April. "I don't know about this."

She was ready for his objections. "One day, Tom. Everything is already baked. Let's try this for one day."

His eyes traveled over the muffins and cookies. He sighed. "Since you cooked everything, we'll sell what you got. Just today."

"Tom, the tourists will be back in a couple weeks. We could make a lot of money serving the muffins for breakfast. And people will be tempted to buy some fudge as they head out."

He shook his head. "Thing is, April, our parents left this shop to both of us, and SueAnne gets a say in everything. If she says no to the muffins, well, it's no muffins"

Reaching her hands into the open back of the cabinet to straighten a doily, April said, "Well, let's see how it goes today. If we make money, maybe SueAnne will change her mind. In the meantime, could you set up the card tables against that wall?"

Looking at the tables and folding chairs stacked neatly in the corner, Tom cocked his head. "Where did those come from?"

"One is Helen's and two belong to the Methodist church. We can use them during the week as long as I get them back on Saturday night."

Tom crossed the room and started unbending the legs on the table. "You sure are a go-getter." He sounded worried.

By noon, every muffin had been sold and the cash register was stuffed with bills. April emerged from the kitchen with a tray of lemon bars, one of Helen's special recipes, and told Tom that she was chilling a batch of chocolate-raspberry fudge. The bell on the door sounded and Roz Penslip, a waitress at The Rudder, walked in. She giggled self-consciously at Tom and April, and said, "Andy told me to come over here and spy. People keep coming in and talking about your muffins."

"What do they say?" April asked.

"Oh, that they're good. Really good."

Smiling at Tom, April lifted her eyebrows and said, "Hear that?"

He opened and closed his mouth twice before saying, "It was April's idea. We're just trying it out for today. It's a one-day thing."

"Oh, I think it's a great idea." Roz said. "Andy's a little sore, but I told him there'll be more business than we can handle in a couple weeks, and it's not like a dozen muffins are going to make or break anybody."

"*See*," April said to Tom. She took two lemon bars from the tray and put them in a bag. "Here, on the house, for you and Andy. We're out of muffins but these are fresh from the oven."

"They smell so good! You know, I've been after Andy for years to sell something besides blueberry muffins. I get so tired of blueberry."

"Tired of blueberry?" Tom interjected, "the tourists buy them by the bagful."

"Yeah, well, we ain't tourists, are we April?"

April broke into a full grin and said, "No way! Come in early tomorrow for a free muffin. One for Andy too." She smiled at Tom.

After Roz left, Tom picked up a lemon bar and took a mouthful. He said, "That's good. I got such a bad feeling about all this."

"Oh, would you stop worrying?" April playfully swatted his arm with a potholder. "Like Roz said, a dozen muffins can't put anyone out of business. You know, I had another idea. We could sell Tasty's T-shirts and postcards. Make money and advertise at the same time."

Tom raised his hands like a traffic cop stopping a car. "Whoa, April, you're going too fast. This is a fudge shop, a little fudge shop. It's been just a little fudge shop for a long, long time."

Walking behind the counter, April said, drawing her syllables out, "Okay, okay. One thing at a time."

"And, April, the muffins? Don't make blueberry. Blueberry's for The Rudder. That's their specialty."

April nodded. "Blueberries are too expensive anyway."

❦   ❦   ❦

For the next week, April was at the shop every day before dawn. She baked, cleaned, and sold the baked goods. "Everything's under control," she told Tom; "go to the bait shop or do whatever else you have to do." He did, and April exulted in being in the shop alone. She made tablecloths for the tables the same shade of peach as her uniform and a new yellow and white gingham valance for the front window. She was working on a new sign advertising tea cakes when the bell rang, causing her to look up as Alice Ransale strode in.

April put her head back down and continued lettering the sign. As she pressed the magic marker to the paper, she asked, "Can I get you something?"

From the way Alice paused before she spoke, April knew she was blowing cigarette smoke from her mouth. "So this is what all the fuss is about," Alice said as she gazed at the cabinet of baked goods.

Walking to the window, April positioned the sign in the corner of the glass. "Fuss? What fuss?"

Alice didn't respond and finally April turned and looked at her. She felt Alice's eyes travel over her from her head to her feet. "You know what fuss." She turned her head quickly and said, "Give me one of those pecan rolls."

"For here or to go?"

Surveying the tables against the wall, Alice said, "Those tablecloths must've cost a pretty penny. There go the profits."

April held the roll with tongs and repeated, "For here or to go?"

Frowning, Alice said, "Just put it in a bag, Missy."

"That's seventy-five cents."

"Put it on my tab," Alice said, turning to walk towards the door.

"I'm sorry but we don't have tabs."

Turning her head over her shoulder, Alice said, "Why, my dear, you most certainly do." She left, the bell sounding twice as the door whacked against its frame.

Immediately, April picked up the magic marker and made another sign, "No Credit." She stared at it for several seconds before crumpling it and tossing it in the garbage.

On Friday, Tom walked in with his fishing rod, a blue sailor's cap unfolded and covering his ears. "SueAnne says we're a fudge shop and to stop with that other stuff."

"Relax," she told him. "Wait till she gets back and sees how well we're doing."

"She wants no part of it, April. Believe me, I've talked to her."

Reaching up, April tugged playfully on both sides of Tom's cap. "People would be disappointed if we stopped selling the baked goods. We have regulars who come in every day." When Tom didn't say anything, April said, "Oh, go fishing. Let's not worry about anything until she's back."

"That's Monday."

"What?"

"SueAnne comes back Monday. It'll be back to business as usual."

April brushed her hands together and said, "Please tell her I'm so happy she's well enough to come back."

After Tom left, April walked into the kitchen. SueAnne will at least be happy about this, April thought. She had organized the cupboards so the pots were neatly stacked, and scoured every inch of surface. There wasn't a granule of sugar on the floor. Looking at the kitchen, April thought, I feel more at home here than I do at Helen's. She felt a wind rush through her body. Her breath flooded her yet she couldn't catch it. This had happened to her once before, the day after her junior year when she had to pack up and go back to Aunt Ginny's house. Then her aunt had given her a glass of water and told her to calm her nerves.

"Aunt Jill, you don't understand . . . Uncle Mel. I can't go back there, please, you know what I mean. You know why . . ." She didn't have enough breath to continue.

Aunt Jill always spoke quickly, everything was matter-of-fact with her.

"April, you're lucky you have a roof over your head. Now this is what we worked out. We've all made sacrifices. To get through life, you make sacrifices."

April cupped her hands under the faucet and then brought them to her cheeks. I'm sick of sacrifices, she thought.

ψ　　　　ψ　　　　ψ

SueAnne came back on Monday. April looked up from the stove and smiled at her. "Welcome back! You look great."

She didn't. SueAnne certainly hadn't lost weight and her skin looked pale and deeply creased.

April smiled and said, "I tried to keep everything clean for you."

SueAnne moved her head about, eyeing the shelves. "Thanks. It looks nice."

Encouraged, April said, "Have a chocolate chip muffin. I used double the chips."

SueAnne pulled her apron over her head and said, "I only eat Andy's muffins." SueAnne waved her hand towards the door. "You can get out front now."

April moved from the stove and said, pleading, "SueAnne, Andy is okay with our selling muffins and stuff. He's fine about it. I don't charge him and—"

Not looking at her, SueAnne said, "Let me get to work."

April grabbed a dish towel, picked up the tin of muffins, and said, "Well, there's no use letting these go to waste." She walked to the front of the shop. The cabinet was already filled with banana muffins and cinnamon cookies. Her regular customers came in and within two hours she had sold the last muffin. She opened the register and counted twenty-three dollars. Six days a week, she added, comes to one hundred and thirty-eight dollars. On a pad, she made some calculations. She tore the page off and spoke as she went to the kitchen, "Okay, hear me out." She went through the swinging door but stopped walking when she felt something gritty beneath her shoe. She looked about and covered her mouth with her hand.

There were pots littered across the counter and the floor was covered with spilled sugar and flour. In the midst of the white ocean were the gingham curtains she'd made to match the valance out front.

"SueAnne!"

She made no indication of having heard April. Leaning over, the large woman examined the fire under a burner, adjusting a knob so the flame grew higher.

"SueAnne, this is ridiculous. We're making a lot of money. Didn't Tom tell you?"

She turned and faced April. The moisture on her face dribbled down her cheeks, and her skin shone a fierce pink. "We sell fudge. We don't step on anybody else's toes."

"But we're not . . . that's not what we're doing."

The bell sounded and SueAnne tilted her head towards the kitchen door. "You got a customer."

❀   ❀   ❀

April was almost asleep that night when she heard a tap on her door. It was Helen letting her know she had a phone call.

She put on her robe and went into the kitchen. "Hello?" she said sleepily.

"Evening, April. It's Tom. Hope I didn't wake you."

"No, no, it's all right."

"Listen, I'm afraid I have some bad news."

"Oh, no. Did SueAnne get sick again?"

"No, no. Nothing like that. She's fine." He waited a moment and said again, "She's fine."

"Oh. That's good." April pressed the phone between her shoulder and chin and tied her robe more tightly. "What's up?"

Tom coughed. "She's feeling fine. But, listen, the thing is, I'm real sorry about this, but I'm afraid we're going to have to let you go."

April was suddenly conscious of how cool the linoleum was beneath her feet. She sat down on a chair. "What? What did you say?"

"Well, summer's just around the corner and SueAnne says she promised Trisha and Nellie they could have their jobs back. See, they've worked for us three summers each and she doesn't think it would be fair."

"Fair?" April's voice echoed, as if she didn't recognize the word.

"Look, I'm sorry April. You did a real good job."

April opened her mouth to speak but swallowed instead. Then she said, "If it's because of the muffins—"

"No," Tom cut her off, "nothing like that. It's just I didn't realize that

SueAnne had promised the girls."

"Do you want me back after Labor Day?"

He hesitated. "I do, but it's no good. My wife. She wants to come back. She's bored at home and feeling lonely. The Avon thing didn't work out. You know how it is."

April nodded but didn't answer. Tom told her he was sorry again and then told her to sleep well.

She laid back down in bed and felt the wind blow wildly through the windows, beating the sheer blue curtains until they seemed to cling to the curtain rod for fear of being ripped off. April shut the windows and climbed back into bed. Her cheeks felt singed, as if both had been slapped.

When the first light fell lazily through the windows, April had been awake for hours wondering where she could possibly find work. She stayed in bed the entire day, not answering Helen's knock. When she ventured into the kitchen, red-eyed, that evening, the older woman hugged her and said, "We'll sell your fudge at Bingo. We'll put that SueAnne right out of business." April smiled weakly and went out to the porch. She saw the glow from Walter's pipe and turned to leave.

"Join me," he called, and April walked to the porch swing. He patted the space next to him but she didn't sit down.

"The victim of your own success, huh? Don't let it get you down. Take that rave review you got and apply for jobs in bakeries in Boston."

"Boston?"

"Yes, Boston. Get out of this provincial little claptrap of a town and enjoy your youth. You should be in a city. A fresh start, that's what you need."

"I like it here."

He exhaled. "Takes all kinds."

"Don't you like it here?"

Shaking his head, he said, "I thought I'd write here. Plays. Dramas," he laughed.

"Did you?"

Rubbing his thumb and forefinger over his eyelids, he shook his head again. "Not a word. Not one single word." He dropped his hand and looked at April. "You know, we could go to Boston together."

"I don't want to go to Boston."

"Think about it. You'll never get another job in this town. You've been blacklisted, kid."

❀   ❀   ❀

The next day, April wrote a flyer and made Xerox copies of it at the post office. Walking up and down the two main streets of Pebbletoe, April posted a copy in every window, on every bulletin board. Finally, she stepped inside Tasty's and handed one to Tom. "Can I post this in your window?" she asked him.

The outsides of his ears reddened, but he said "Sure. Good luck, April." He glanced toward the kitchen door and April understood that she shouldn't linger. Tom went behind the counter and punched the cash register. He removed two twenty dollar bills and said, "Here, you take this. And you'll get your last check on Friday." April stared at the top bill; someone had written "Sugar" on it in blue ink.

She walked out of the shop and down the street. Every window she passed displayed her ad: "Au Pair for hire. Available immediately." Helen's phone number was listed below. She knew the tourists would call her, that they'd let her take care of their children for a week or maybe two. They'd take her to dinner and ask her about her life. They would show her every kindness and every insult before they went away. Then what? She didn't want to leave. This was her home. Maybe she could earn enough from the tourists so she could stay through the year.

April walked to the ocean, the breeze blowing against her becoming stronger and stronger as she approached the edge of the water. She stood in the wet sand, her toes sinking, and squared her shoulders against the wind. Still, it pushed at her, rocking her back on her heels, as if trying with all its might to push her over. As the sun dipped lower, the sand cooled. Scooping it with her hands, April became mesmerized with the feel of it spilling between her fingers, grainy but silky, each speck a tiny resident of the beach.

SISTERLY

My sister is schizophrenic. That's the medical term. Most people would just say she's crazy. Whenever I complain about LeeAnne, my mother says, "You can't expect her to behave like other people, Eva. She has a mental illness." As if I could forget. These last three years, since I started high school, have been absolute hell with my sister moving in and out of the house, going on and off medications, and in and out of treatment centers. Her life is on permanent replay.

Sometimes she disappears for days on end only to reappear and insist she was with Jim Morrison, the rock star who's been dead some forty years. She says she and Jim sail in his crystal ship through galaxies not yet charted by the scientists. When I ask her if she got seasick, she thinks I'm being serious and explains that they sail through *time*, "from his past to my present." As bad as all that is, I could handle it and be sympathetic, agree with my mother that, yes, my sister can't be held responsible for her actions because she's sick, but it's the *way* she's sick that's so fucking embarrassing. She's so public about it. The whole world knows she's schizophrenic because of the crazy blog she writes, "LeeAnne On The Other Side," where she regularly announces to the world that she's "The Lizard King's wife." Not his widow, mind you, his *wife*. LeeAnne insists, "Death is no match for our love. Jim can break on through to me at any moment." Ain't no mountain high enough and ain't no paranormal dimension thick enough, I guess. She plays The Doors non-stop but it all sounds like Twilight Zone music to me.

You should never try to wrestle a delusion from a mentally ill person, so her doctors tell us over and over, but when LeeAnne holds forth on how she came to believe she was a dead rock star's wife, I want to turn down her volume. "*I* live in Los Angeles. My name is *LeeAnne*, my initials are *L* and *A*. *LA Woman!* Get it? He wrote that for me. For *me!*" she finishes, slapping her chest. It does no good to point out that she was named for our parents, Lee and Anne. And don't tell her that she isn't the only person with those initials, that there are probably many women in Los Angeles with those initials. Logic is useless to my sister; she'll tell you you're the crazy one. There are days I think I am.

Many people read the blog because LeeAnne is a little bit famous. That's the wrong word. Infamous (I'm studying for the SAT), she's rather infamous since *The Los Angeles Times* published her letter to the editor demanding that "my husband's body" be exhumed from Père Lachaise and reburied here in Forest Lawn. Why? So she could buy the plot next to his, so they could be eternally united. Then she retracted her statement in another letter declaring that "An imposter's body lies in my husband's grave in Paris. No one but me, his wife and one true love, knows where he's really buried. The truth is he's buried in my heart." She thinks her words are deep, so profound that they shock people and then cause them to revere her. She doesn't understand why news cameras aren't following her around, why journalists aren't lining up to interview her. "People look at me," she insists. "They look at me because they know I'm Jim's wife, his eternal love. They see his aura." She circles her head with her hand. "It surrounds me like a blue halo." I wonder what color surrounds me when I'm with her. My face was scarlet when she told a clerk in a record store, "String theorists should be studying me. I'm consciously living parallel lives."

The blue bus she has tattooed on her upper chest is massive, and Lee-Anne dresses to reveal its entirety. Every now and then, some Doors fan strikes up a conversation about the tattoo, about what it means in that song, and LeeAnne can't wait to enlighten him that the song is about *her*, about Jim Morrison embracing the end of his life because he didn't find her waiting for him at the back of the blue bus. When they walk away from her, LeeAnne thinks she's made another convert. Some of them say, "Oh, you're *that* chick," and she doesn't get that they're staring at her like a freak, that they realize she's the woman who wrote the letters to the paper, or that maybe they've read her blog. No, LeeAnne thinks they can't believe their good fortune, being in her presence. LeeAnne's cover of Morrison's death is that he didn't accidentally OD in Paris; no, he committed suicide so "he could find me on the other side." So why were you born? Why didn't you just stay on the other side with him? I learned to stop asking questions. The answers never make any sense. Being LeeAnne's sister is like listening to old vinyl records that are scratched to hell. You can't hear the lyrics any more but the static is so thick it scars your ears.

I wish I didn't have to read her blog but I learned the hard way that I need to know every bizarre thing LeeAnne writes. There are a couple bitchy girls at school who pretend to be all concerned about her, blinking their dyed eyelashes when they say things like, "Eva, I hope your sister is getting help. Have you read her latest post?" That would be yesterday's entry: *I sent a long letter to* Rolling Stone *letting them know that I'm Jim Morrison's wife and eternal time-traveling companion. I told them I'm available for an interview, no payment necessary, as long as I'm on the cover. My cell phone should be ringing any time now. After the interview appears, I'll undoubtedly go on the talk show circuit. Soon the whole world will know of Jim's enormous, eternal love for me, LeeAnne Morrison.*

Of course I cringe when I read this crap but the posts people write in response are beyond vicious. There are two regulars who post under the names "NirvanaNow" and "Serpent666." NirvanaNow always trashes the pictures of herself LeeAnne posts, saying she's "so ugly, no way Morrison would ever have given her a second look." That pisses me off. LeeAnne used to be pretty, not drop-dead gorgeous or anything, but pretty. The medicine she takes, when she really takes it and doesn't just pretend to, throws off her metabolism and makes her gain weight. When her weight is up, she tries to distract from it with make-up but she wears way too much and it makes her skin break out. Serpent666 chimes in with things like, "Hate to disappoint you but *I* am Morrison's wife. He thinks you're batshit crazy."

And then, a couple months ago, there was a poster named "RiderontheStorm" who claimed to *be* Jim Morrison. He was feeding LeeAnne lines like, "Keep the faith, my love. I'm always with you. I live for the hour we're together again." LeeAnne was ecstatic. "He's found a portal to speak to me!" Oh, I wanted to kill that poster, making a nutty woman even nuttier. After a few weeks of pretending to be Morrison, he posted, "Lady, you're fucking crazy. I've been yanking your chain and you believed it all. Get help. Fast."

I hoped that would put an end to the blog but after crying for days, Lee-Anne posts: *So many people are jealous of Jim's love for me, they'll do anything to try to destroy it. Jim has told me to be strong and ignore the haters. He's here, right now, protecting me, loving me, and there's nothing you motherfuckers can do about it.*

She's right. There isn't.

I'm in love too but with a living, breathing person. Nick and I have been together for three months. After our first date in early summer, a walk around Elysian Park, he emailed me a haiku:

You are the big wind
That blows open my petals
And stirs my stamen.

My heart is kinder than my brain. Nick couldn't write poetry but these novice, obvious lines meant more to me than a Shakespearean sonnet. I emailed him back:

Your hand reached beyond
My grateful fingers to clasp
Newly rising sun.

Nick asked me what it meant. "The sun wasn't rising. It was afternoon, remember?" So, he wasn't the brightest but being literal can be a good thing. He'd never hide behind a metaphor or imagine anything that couldn't pass a reality test. I typed back, "I guess I lost track of time." That part was true.

We met because of LeeAnne. I got a message on Facebook from him out of the blue: *Hi, we don't know each other but I saw on Facebook that you're friends with LeeAnne? You have the same last name and you kind of look like a junior version of her so maybe you two are sisters? Anyways I'm messaging you because I don't know what to do. Someone told me about her blog, "LeeAnne on the other side" and I took a look. Man, there's some pretty out there stuff on that page. She thinks she's married to Jim Morrison and time and space don't exist, yada, yada. I don't care what anyone believes, her business, but she said a couple things that scare me. Like all this stuff about the final breakthrough where she doesn't come back to the 21st century, that she stays permanently with Morrison in 1970. She says sometime soon they'll finally be together. I mean, I hope she's not going to off herself. Sorry. That can't be fun to hear. But anyways, short of calling the police, I didn't know what to do. Maybe you can help her. If you can't, maybe someone else? Like her mom?*

I was just going to respond, "Yes, my sister's crazy. Good-bye," but then I looked at his Facebook page picture and saw this skinny, short guy with bed-head hair and a chipped front tooth. Eyes that made me crave Oreo cookies. He was a couple years older than me, out of high school, and he listed his occupation as "artist." The background on his page was a photo of a painting he'd done, a painting with a drooping, misshapen heart about to fall from the top of a streetlamp. The heart was just hanging on for dear life, even as it was slipping away, and the streetlamp was just loving the heart with all its might, shining its light on the heart because that was all it could do. It's like the lamp was saying, "Look, this isn't what you need, I know, but it's all I've got, and I can't just stand here and not even try." The painting is why I didn't just write Nick off. Don't get me wrong, there wasn't a hint of refined technique or even raw talent in the picture. No, any kid could've painted it, but the picture was just so damn simple and honest. I started looking at streetlamps and wondering how many hearts they'd seen fall. In the same world, there's people like NirvanaNow and Serpent666, calling my sister a "delusional bitch," and then there's people like Nick, looking for a way to help. He didn't know there was no way to help LeeAnne. For Nick, life was still fixable.

❋   ❋   ❋

LeeAnne first got sick when she was away at college, when I was still in middle school. In her second year at Stanford, she called home and told Dad that one of her professors had kicked her out of his literature class for "exposing the inconsistencies of his insipid deconstruction of Milton." LeeAnne had graduated from high school in two and a half years and had a pretty hefty scholarship to Stanford from a foundation that supported female high-achievers. Our parents were so proud, especially Dad. He has a master's in English from San Francisco State but was never able to do anything with it other than adjunct teaching. He gave that up to work in advertising, a job with health benefits and, he says, "ample humiliation." Mom teaches English at a private high school in Glendale. She describes her students as "over-privileged and ungrateful." The two of them were sure getting a PhD from a top school would give LeeAnne a floor seat at the academic show that they so wanted for themselves.

When LeeAnne broke the news about being dismissed from class, Dad was on the phone with Stanford within moments. When he hung up, I saw the fear in his face, like that time he'd gotten stung by a bee and had to use the EpiPen pen he carries with him. LeeAnne had been suspended from Stanford and could not be readmitted without a mental health evaluation. When Mom started sputtering questions, Dad looked at her, his voice as thin as a thread being pulled through a needle and said, "She took her shirt off in his class."

"*What?*" Mom's voice was a gunshot in my ear. "You mean . . . you mean she was just . . . in her bra?" She walked around Dad, positioning herself in front of him so he had to meet her gaze.

He barely shook his head, as if any real movement would make things even worse. "No bra." Swallowing, his Adam's apple lowering then rising, he said, "She exposed herself."

Mom pushed at the sides of her face. "What was she thinking?! How could she do that?"

Dad looked at me. "Do you know anything?"

I shook my head. I was almost five years younger than LeeAnne. Our lives didn't overlap, not for a long time, anyway.

"Has she ever said anything to you about a difficult professor?" Dad looked at me like he thought I was keeping a secret. "About a professor that maybe tried to flirt with her? Or . . ."

"No."

"Nothing?" Mom's voice was accusing. "Eva, she must've said *something*. When she was home for Christmas? You sleep in the same room. *Think!*"

I shrugged. "She didn't say anything." My parents stood, spellbound, and I went to my room.

❦   ❦   ❦

Once upon a time, long, long ago, my sister and I were close. At night, when I was about three or four, LeeAnne used to sit next to me in bed and read picture books. She'd put her finger under the words and patiently sound them out and have me repeat them. I liked that but not nearly as much as the stories she made up, wonderful stories that I begged to hear again and again. There was a special one about a butterfly with my name, Eva, who lived in a beautiful garden. The butterfly had all kinds of adventures. She could talk to the flowers, the "sugar blossoms," and they answered in a sing-song voice, "Eva, come dance on our petals." Eva called bees "the buzzy boys" and liked to have flying races with them through trees swimming with "the leaf girls in their green dresses." Always, toward the end of the story, a mischievous little boy would try to pick all of the flowers but no matter how hard he pulled, they remained rooted to the ground. Eva would then open her wings to their fullest and fly to the tallest treetop. "This is my garden," she said, "and no harm will come to any of my friends who live here." Then she flew around the garden and somehow created an invisible gate that would keep the little boy out forever. The butterfly, the bees, the flowers, and the leaf girls were happy and safe "for always and always." I would add one more "And always," just to make sure it was really true.

When did all that change? Maybe when LeeAnne was in fifth grade and a teacher told mom her daughter was "more than gifted." I remember bragging to my friends that "My sister is a *real* genius." Sometimes they'd ask me if I was, and I just shook my head. I wasn't embarrassed; one genius per family seemed about right. But I think it was about then that LeeAnne started yelling at me not to touch her stuff. The bedtime stories stopped. She was constantly reading thick books and telling me not to make a sound, to let her concentrate. She wrote things down in dozens of notebooks that stacked up in her bookcase. When she was in high school, she was often away at debating tournaments, her winning ribbons tossed in a cardboard box under her bed or used as bookmarks. Then LeeAnne was gone. Off to college and out of my life. That's what I thought since she left for Stanford but then the story changed. LeeAnne came home. And she brought Jim Morrison with her. Not exactly the college roommate Mom had hoped for her daughter.

Nick doesn't have a studio. I'm posing for him in his parents' garage. It's hotter than hell because it's July, and he has the door down because I'm naked. A slanted shaft of light from the side window crosses the concrete floor where I stand holding an old doll of mine, a big one with no hair, in front of me. My arms are getting heavy but Nick keeps saying, "Just a little bit longer, a little bit more, hang in there, you look so beautiful, don't move . . ."

"Are you going to make the doll look like a real baby?"

"No. It's a doll."

"I know it's a doll but are you going to paint it as a doll or a baby?"

"If I was going to paint a baby, I'd have you hold a baby."

"Where would we get one?"

"Oh. Good point."

When I laugh, I break the pose. My arms need to rest and I want to see what the painting looks like.

"No, not yet!" Nick protests as I walk to him but he doesn't stop me. It's hard to describe what I see on the canvas. My hair, real long and thick, sprouts out behind the baby's head like Medusa's snakes. Then there's the baby's limbs entangled in my arms, both of us a pinky beige, and my breasts on either side of the baby's chest. The whole thing is a sad mess but I say, "Wow! This is so cool!"

"Yeah?" Nick's chipped tooth bites his lower lip when he smiles.

I'm such a liar. "Yeah, it's awesome."

"What does it say to you?"

Oh, God. Staring at the painting, I start by describing it. "Well, the doll is in front of the real person."

"Yeah."

"So it's like the real person is saying, 'Look society, you don't want me, you want who you think I am. You just want this doll so you can project whatever you think and feel onto it."

"Yeah! That's what I was going for."

"It's quite a statement."

Nick's gaze flickers from me to the painting and back again. "Yeah, it is. A statement. You know, that's a good name for this, 'Statement.'" He points at the painting with both index fingers. "And then, like, if I do another one, that one will be 'Statement Two.'"

I can't keep my eyebrows from lifting but I say quickly, "Sure. You could do a whole series."

He cups his hands over my breasts and I pull his face toward mine. He's not even a full inch taller than me and I'm short. His kisses taste like the candy fireballs he sucks on to keep from smoking because he doesn't want to stunt his growth. How can I tell him it's already too late?

There's an old sheet on the floor to protect the concrete from paint. It's spotted with bits of the portrait, bits of me. We move down onto it. Through the worn fabric, my back feels the hard concrete floor. Nick is so gentle with me, though, it feels like I'm up in the air, cradled in some frothy, foaming cloud. It feels like this every time, like we've discovered the simple secret to flying. I love his racing breath on my neck, his tongue tracing my lips until I can't stand it and have to kiss him back and tell him to get inside me, to make me feel like we're soaring together. If LeeAnne could feel *this*, even once, she'd know that all her words about time travel with Jim Morrison are just a fantasy. Because this moment with Nick, it's everything good about life and it's *now*. I don't want to be anywhere else, only here, in the garage, the dusky light catching Nick's eyes so his pupils shrink, sink back into those black-as-night irises and almost disappear. It's only a moment but somehow it's forever too. This happiness, it's so big, it could suffocate me.

In the middle of my summer with Nick, LeeAnne seems better. Well, better in some ways. She's on new meds that make her really sleepy. She's never up in the morning and she just lies around the house in the afternoon. She doesn't say much when we eat dinner. She doesn't eat much either but tonight she sticks her fingernail in the butter and peels ribbons of it off. Then she sucks on it, her eyes closed like she's really savoring it. Mom starts to tell her to stop but Dad taps her hand and she doesn't finish. They've been so hopeful since LeeAnne started the new meds. She hasn't said a word about you-know-who and she hasn't snuck out of the house. Last night, Mom and Dad even took a walk after dinner, left LeeAnne home alone for a half-hour. But tonight, after my parents leave the table, she scrapes several rows of butter and rubs it into her bus tattoo. I risk a joke: "So it's not the blue bus, it's the butter bus?" She doesn't answer.

That night, hours after midnight, both of us sleeping in our room, I hear LeeAnne say in a heartbroken whisper, "Is this all in my head? Did I make it all up?"

Yes! I scream in my own head but I pretend I haven't woken up.

"Jim? Jim, are you here? Jim, don't leave me!"

Maybe I should go to her. But then she whispers, "Don't leave me here with these people, Jim. They're not my family. You're my family, Jim. You, only you!" Now her voice sounds hissing.

I want to scream, "I'm your sister! Mom and Dad are your parents!" But what good would it do? I'm so sick of this crap. My parents have been through this so many times and they're so tired. We're all exhausted. I close my eyes and pray that LeeAnne is done calling out to Jim Morrison for the night. She must be because I fall asleep.

The next morning, LeeAnne is gone.

"Where do you think she went?" Nick asks.

"Who knows? We never really know where she goes when she takes off. When she comes back, she always says that she was with Jim Morrison. Can I steal a French fry?"

Nick slides his plate across the table. "Help yourself."

We're at a little diner in Silver Lake where Nick used to wash dishes when he was in high school. He's a part-time short-order cook at another place not too far from here. "Someone at the Los Feliz Public Library called my mom yesterday and told her a girl was there cutting up old newspapers. The security guard made her leave. That might've been LeeAnne."

Squeezing zigzag lines of ketchup onto the plate, Nick says, "How'd the librarian know to call your mother?"

"Oh, my mother goes places to see if anyone has seen LeeAnne. Libraries, laundromats, churches. You know, places where people can hang out without being hassled too much."

"Sure." Nick puts his forearms on the table and his smile seems teasing, his tongue touching the bottom of that chipped tooth. "Hey, I have to tell you something. It's big."

"Yeah?"

He nods fast, excited, but he holds the news in for a few seconds, really makes me wait. Then, in a rush, "I'm moving to San Francisco!"

My eyelids shut and open a few times. "San Francisco?" I say, more loudly than I meant to. Nicks eyes widen and he laughs and says, "Hey, lower the volume." The waitress stops at our table and refills our glasses with Coke. I can't believe that after announcing to me that he's moving, leaving me, Nick turns to the waitress and says, "Say, could I have more ice?"

There's a tiny mountain in my throat, its sharp little peak digging into my soft palate. I try to swallow but the mountain seems to take root down to my stomach." I ask him, "When?" Then I ask what should have been my first question, "Why?"

The waitress is back with a small glass of ice that she tips into Nick's drink. Looking at her, he says, "Thanks," and immediately lifts the glass to his mouth and starts crunching some ice like he's trying to chip another tooth.

"Nick?"

He burps loudly and claps his hand over his mouth. Smiling, he says, "Wow, carbonation. Excuse me." Making a fist, he thumps his chest a few times. "Okay, I'm good now. I just think it's time. I've decided I want to paint, I mean *really* paint." He lifts his hands and drops them onto the table, "and my cousin's got a little place in North Beach. He and his roommates, they all work in an art supply store and they all paint when they're not working."

"Paint? Paint what? Houses?"

He throws his head back and laughs. "No, silly! They're artists. Like me."

Like Nick?

"So, next weekend, I'm going to take the bus up."

"And?"

He pours some salt in a blob of ketchup, slides his finger through it, and puts it to his tongue. The gesture makes me think of LeeAnne and the butter. I shake my head to make the image go away.

Nick talks on so nonchalantly, like he's telling me the plot of a movie he saw. "Ronnie will meet me at the station and we'll head over to the apartment. I just need to bring some clothes. He says they've got a sleeping bag. And some wood to make an easel."

An easel. Make an easel and *presto*! You're an artist. I circle my dry lips with the tip of my tongue and say, "This is crazy!"

Looking at me, his mouth partly open, Nick says, "Why?"

"Well, I thought I'd get more than a week's notice. I mean . . . what about us?"

There's a flash of understanding on his face as he finally connects the dots. "Oh, oh, Eva. I'm sorry. Oh, God, you must think I'm a jerk."

Whew. There's an explanation. Something that will make sense out of all of this. Nick's not the brightest, but he is the sweetest. He touches my arm, his fingers teasing the little hairs, and I feel a shiver. "You can come visit. You can come any time," he says. "Well, I guess I have to check with Ronnie to see if you can stay with us but if it's just for a couple nights, he won't care."

I study the pattern in the linoleum. Aqua and lime green tiles with a lot of grime in the seams. "Don't we love each other?" My voice is low now, broken.

He scoops both of my hands into his. "Hey, hey, of course we do." When he presses my fingers to his lips, I think how awful life would be without him. My distraught parents, the bitchy girls at school. Nick made it all bearable. He clears his throat and says, "But I'm too young to get engaged or anything. You understand that."

"Engaged? I'm not even eighteen!"

"Exactly," he says, like I'm following his twisted logic. He has ketchup in a corner of his mouth. He looks younger than me, like such a kid.

"But . . . well, we're in love. Doesn't that mean something?"

"Oh, hey, of course it does," he says, like he's trying to calm me down. "Eva, you've helped me become a better artist. I will be grateful to you forever. But, San Francisco, it's like . . . my dream, my biggest dream, to be an artist there."

"Why in San Francisco?"

And then he starts crunching ice again. I can feel the cubes grinding in my temples, the *grruum-grruum* sound jack-hammering between them. He says, "It's a better scene for artists. Los Angeles, I think it holds me back. Everything here is like too slick, you know? Too commercial. I need a new landscape. Some place fresh. Some place where I can really lose myself in my art, you know?" He looks at me like he's said something beautiful, like I too must be in awe of his words.

I inhale and say as plainly as I can, "Nick, you can't paint. You don't have the first clue about painting."

Setting down his drink, he says, "Hey, that's low, really low. I know you don't want me to go, but that's just mean."

I shake my head and lock eyes with him. "It would be mean if I *didn't* tell you. I should have told you before. No real painter in San Francisco, or anywhere, is going to take you seriously."

"Then why'd you tell me I was awesome, huh?" He points his chin out over the table, challenging me. "You're just saying this because I'm leaving."

Clenching my fingers around the curve of the booth's seat, I say quietly, "You paint like you're in elementary school, like some kid who's just gotten past finger painting."

Nick swings his legs to the side of the booth and stands up. "What do you know? Your sister's fucking crazy." He walks out the door as the waitress puts the check on the table and says, "When you're ready."

❦   ❦   ❦

LeeAnne has never stayed away this long. My mother spends every spare minute calling hospitals and homeless shelters. I wonder if she's going to start posting flyers around Los Angeles with LeeAnne's picture on it. You see pictures of lost animals all the time, cats and dogs that just wander off and get lost, or maybe someone takes them in and feeds them. It bothers me to think that my sister, too, has just wandered off and now is a stray person somewhere in this sprawling city. It's so weird but I can't stop humming that Doors' song, "L.A. Woman." Now Jim Morrison does seem to be singing about my sister, a lost angel in this big, black city of night.

Mom is pissed that Dad isn't helping her. When he comes home from work, he sits on the couch for hours doing Sudoku puzzles. He's getting good, faster at figuring out which number goes in which square. There's a pile of puzzle books he's already done on the coffee table. I'm not mad at him. It's his way to get through this.

I can't tell my parents that part of me is relieved. Oh, I get panicked now and then, for sure, but these days with no blog posts are a nice break. When I run into my bitchy classmates at the mall, they have nothing to say. But as more and more days go by, panic starts building in my lungs, brick by brick. It's a strain to breathe sometimes and it has nothing to do with smog.

I doze on and off but my short dreams are visions of LeeAnne under a car or in the back of an ambulance or being strangled by some maniac. Her absence feels different these last few days. Emptier, somehow. I know that this time she won't come back. One morning, three weeks after she left, I get out of bed at dawn, dress, and then walk outside to get the newspaper. I'm heading back into the house when Mom opens the door and steps onto the porch. I know it's over. There's no movement in the air and the moment goes on and on. The past, the present, and the future are all stitched up together. I go to Mom and we hang onto each other. Holding her cheek against mine, she whispers, "LeeAnne was in a storage locker in Encinitas. Dad is going to the police station to identify the body."

"Are they absolutely sure it's her?"

Her face barely moves when she nods. "The locker was filled with pictures of Jim Morrison. And, you know, the bus tattoo."

"Oh, God, yeah." How dumb of me to forget that.

"Pills. She took pills. She probably just fell asleep. It was probably very peaceful."

Now Mom slides her arms around me and our shoulders sway slowly together. "The man who called said she rented the locker last spring. No one realized that she was staying overnight these last few weeks. Rent was overdue so they opened the locker to clean it out."

I don't ask but I know we're both thinking about LeeAnne's body. How long has she been dead? The storage locker, all those pictures of a dead man. She was already in a tomb.

❦   ❦   ❦

It's odd but I feel better lying on LeeAnne's bed. There's a warmth here and maybe an energy too, soft and peaceful. Well, maybe it's just the chenille bed cover, I don't know. I like to look at some of the things she kept from childhood and her teen years, things that meant something to her before she got sick. Hair ribbons and old bottles of perfume, books and LeeAnne's own notebooks filled with stories, poetry, and sketches. As I page through an old spiral-bound one with a red cover, I see lots of pencil etchings of humming-birds, butterflies, and flowers. She drew such happy, pretty pictures before she got sick.

I turn a page and find a self-portrait, a picture of my sister with tears on her cheeks. Above her head are caption clouds, the kind you seen in cartoons, but all three of them are empty. When did she draw this? I wonder if I should show it to my parents. My mother hasn't set foot in this room since we got the phone call. I rest my index finger on one of the sketched tears in the drawing and gently rub it back and forth.

Flipping through the final pages of the notebook, I find a poem with the title, "Sister."

> *She was not first but she is Eva*
> *May she never know these fears*
> *These moments when she thinks*
> *She may be hearing a voice*
> *In a room so quiet that the sound*
> *Of swallowing her own saliva*
> *Thunders in her confused ears.*
> *The voice that is seducing me*
> *May it never tempt her.*

So, the dead can talk to us after all. LeeAnne. She was no ordinary sister. She never yelled at me for borrowing a sweater or gave me advice about boys, typical big sister things. But she did worry that I'd end up like her. That's a different kind of caring. I gulp to swallow the sob creeping up my throat. I wish I could thank LeeAnne for, in her own way, being sisterly. Sisterly in a way most people could never understand.

The blog. LeeAnne hadn't written anything for a few days before she disappeared so it hasn't been updated for weeks. When I log in, I see NirvanaNow and Serpent666 have been having a conversation:

"Hey, where is she? Is she gone?"

"Dunno. Hope not. This site is funny as shit."

"Maybe she got back on her meds. That'd be a shame."

That's as far as I read. Such assholes.

Setting my fingers on the keyboard, I type: "A few weeks ago, LeeAnne Morrison broke through to the other side where she was joined by her husband, Jim Morrison. They live and love in paradise for eternity."

I will never log in to see what the assholes think of this. LeeAnne is free now; she has flown from this world to the top of a garden where she is happy and safe, and there's nothing these motherfuckers can do about it. Not a damn thing.

MUTUAL

"They're real young," the landlady said as she handed Liz the keys. "Maybe nineteen or twenty. They have a baby named Amber Dawn, isn't that pretty? Oh, but she doesn't make any noise. Diane tells me she's a real good sleeper. You won't hear a thing."

The woman looked at her watch, a large black circle held by two strips of neon pink vinyl. "Well, I better be going. Just remember, you split water and electricity with them. Diane will come up with the bill each month. I've only met Ron a couple times. Not real talkative. Oh, and if I need to get in touch with you during the day, I should call the college?"

"Yes. Call the college switchboard and ask for the French department. How much do water and electricity cost each month?"

"Oh, not much, I'm sure. Just ask Diane. Well, I hope you like it here. There aren't too many young folks in town. It'll sure be a change from Chicago for you."

Liz watched the landlady drive off in her rusted orange Firebird, the muffler coughing as she veered around the corner. Walking up to the house, Liz noticed two black metal mailboxes affixed to the white siding. The top one, hers, was unmarked. The bottom one had a piece of white paper taped to it with the words "Bemerly - Downstairs" written in oily black marker.

Diane came up the next day to make sure Liz understood about the utilities. She told Liz that since Mrs. Sandell, the landlady, paid for heat, not to be afraid to crank the thermostat as high as she wanted. Then Diane talked about her baby and her husband, not much else. She didn't work and most of her friends were like her, at home with a baby or two. She asked politely if Liz liked her job, and then grinned shyly and said, "Are there cute, young professors to date?" Liz laughed, at last some familiar girl talk, and told her no, there weren't.

Not that Liz was looking that hard. She had started dating Michael, a lawyer, a couple of months before she left Chicago. Her best friend Sara, also a lawyer, had introduced them. Things had been going well, very well, she thought, when DePaul University cut Liz's position because of budget constraints. The job market was bleak; she had been lucky to find a position in southeastern Indiana at Saint Peter's, a small liberal arts college.

Now, aside from long distance phone calls, Diane's visits were about the extent of her social life. Liz was entertained, in a way, by Diane's lack of sophistication and simple interests, her absorption with perming her hair or trying out a new shade of eye make-up. Not that they'd ever be friends or anything, they had nothing in common, but Liz found she liked talking to Diane. She was lonely for her friends in Chicago, and the faculty at this podunk college weren't likely prospects for friends. A colleague in the French department had asked her if she'd like to sell Mary Kay cosmetics in her spare time, and an older man in the English department had invited her to join his Bible study group. Liz had politely declined, but asked herself, *where the hell am I?* She occasionally went to a mall, a half-hour's drive away, and walked around and had dinner at a pizzeria. She poured over the job ads in the Chicago newspapers wondering if she should settle for teaching high school. She was under contract for the full academic year at St. Peter's College, but she promised herself that by the start of summer, she'd have a new job lined up in Chicago.

Only once did Diane bring Ron up with her to meet Liz. He had shrugged his shoulders and mumbled, "Let me know if you have trouble with your car."

"He can fix *anything!*" Diane exclaimed.

Later, Liz chortled as she talked with Sara on the phone. "I can't believe how I stared at him! He's the best-looking guy in town. God help me, I've got to get out of these cornfields!"

It was an opening for Sara to mention Michael, who hadn't called in several days, not since Liz had suggested that she visit him Columbus Day weekend. But Sara changed the subject and told Liz about a difficult embezzlement case she was working on. Liz couldn't bring herself to openly ask about Michael, scared that Sara might blab to their mutual friends that Liz was pining away for him in Indiana.

Liz thought about calling Michael, did in fact leave a buoyant, "Hey, stranger, what's happening?" message on his answering machine, and felt humiliated when he didn't call back. A week later, she received a brief note in the mail. Michael hoped she was well, but he didn't see a future for their relationship given the distance factor. Liz tried calling Sara several times. She wanted to sound relaxed, maybe casually mention a fictitious professor who was unabashedly pursuing her. Something to be repeated to Michael. Sara didn't answer her phone. Liz was not totally surprised when, a week later, she found a letter from Sara in her mailbox. She scanned it as she leaned against the side of the house. The clichés slid into one rambling apology: *Neither one of us intended this to happen, we never meant to hurt you, hope you'll understand, can we still be friends?* Enclosed with the letter was a photo of Liz and Sara taken the previous year. The two women were standing with their arms around each other in Grant Park

Liz folded the picture over and over until it was too small to crease one more time. She walked down the street, watching the cornfields at the end of it become larger and larger as she approached. The upright stalks and husks were burnt a faded brittle yellow, all but begging for harvest. Liz lifted her arm and flung the picture into the field and imagined it shredded by a huge tractor in a few weeks.

At home, she wrote Sara a hurried reply filled with reverse clichés: Don't be silly, Michael and I were never serious, my best to both of you, too busy to write more now, more later.

Liz tried not to think about the betrayal but it sat on the surface of her mind like a beach ball on water, unable to be pushed beneath the surface. Images of Michael and Sara together were impossible to repress, bobbing up while she was driving to work and teaching her classes. Worse, there was no one to talk to about it. Other friends in Chicago who might've reached out to her didn't. When Diane stopped up with the bill, Liz briefly mentioned that she and Michael had broken up.

"Gosh, I'm sorry." she said. "His loss, huh?"

"Right," Liz said, looking over the utilities bill.

"Don't worry. You'll meet someone else. Before Ron and I got married, I got dumped by this guy who sold corn seed for Henderson Acres. I thought I'd die." Diane rolled her head back and looked up at the ceiling to exaggerate her words. "But see, I got over it. You will too."

Liz's chest swelled and she said, as if addressing students in a class, "Well, I don't know how alike Michael and your corn salesman are, but we're both better off without them."

Missing her point, Diane nodded emphatically. "Right."

Liz looked at Diane's face, full of compassion and so attentive, and felt a sob constrict her throat. "Do you want to see a movie sometime?" she blurted.

❀   ❀   ❀

The semester wore on. Winter came early, the first snow falling on Halloween. Shivering, Liz stood on the sidewalk with Diane and Ron and handed out packaged candy to the children going door to door in their costumes. Liz took several photos of Amber in the pumpkin costume Diane had made. She got them developed and put the cutest one in a frame. When she saw it, Diane exclaimed, "Ron thinks all the people at the college are stuck up but I told him you're different!"

November was dreary. Now that the cornfields surrounding the town were bare, the chilling wind whistled through the streets. The sun was forever behind the clouds, the town dressed from dawn to dusk in a gray haze. Liz hibernated, staying home on weekends and drinking hot coffee as she sat on the couch under a pile of blankets watching television. She started smoking again, a habit she had quit after college, and lost her appetite. There were weekends when she spoke to no one, the sound of her own voice startling her in class on Monday mornings. In her apartment, she welcomed the sound of Amber crying downstairs. It was the only noise she heard besides the television. Driving the few miles to and from the college, stopping for groceries and gas, was the only time she spent outdoors. One afternoon before Thanksgiving, she stopped to fill her tank and noticed a picture of Amber in her pumpkin costume taped to one of the gas pumps. When Ron came out, she pointed to it, smiling, and he said, "My baby gets me through the day. People always tell me she's so cute." How sweet, Liz thought, but she realized that a few months ago, she would have found this strange.

Liz tried to extend Diane's visits, offering her Pepsi or coffee, but Diane was not as talkative these days. There was always laundry to fold or Amber was cranky and ready for a nap. One Saturday afternoon in early December, however, Diane agreed to a soda. They went into the living room and sat on the couch. Liz had been preparing a lesson; an intermediate French textbook sat on the coffee table opened to a chapter on irregular verbs. Diane noticed it and flipped through a few pages. "I took two years of French in high school," she said. "If I went to college, maybe I would've majored in it."

"Did you think of going to college?"

"No, not really, not after I met Ron."

"How did you meet? Did you go to high school together?"

"Yeah, we did, but I didn't know him that well then. It was after gradu- ation. I was riding around the cornfields off Route 14 one night with my girlfriends. We ran into him and his buddies. They were drinking and smok- ing pot." She shook her head but smiled a little. "I couldn't believe it when he asked me out. I never would've thought I could get a guy like Ron."

"Why? You're pretty!" Liz wondered if she sounded convincing.

"Oh," Diane looked at the floor and smiled, "thanks, but I wasn't the prettiest in my class and a lot of girls liked Ron." She looked at Liz and smiled shyly, her very pointed eyeteeth pressing into her lower lip. "But I knew something about him that they didn't."

"What?"

"I knew he liked kids. He helped out with a Little League team my nephew was on. I saw the way he was with the little boys. Patient, you know? He didn't yell at them like other coaches do."

"That's nice."

"Yeah. I wasn't scared to tell him I was pregnant. I mean, I let him do it a few times when he didn't have a condom, so it wasn't a big surprise." Diane pulled her lips in and closed her eyes.

"How long have you been married?" Liz asked softly, anticipating some- thing.

"Almost a year and a half," Diane answered. Cupping her hand over her mouth, she lowered her head towards the floor and started to rock back and forth. Gulping for air, a tear sliding down each cheek, she said, "We got married on my eighteenth birthday."

"Hey, don't cry. What's wrong? Tell me."

"It's just, well, I'm sure it's crazy, but he's never home now." Diane turned side-ways, crossing her legs, and sank her upper body against the back of the couch. "My friend Sharlene thinks he's sleeping with someone."

"Who?" Liz asked abruptly, surprising herself. She lifted a box of tissues off the coffee table and Diane pulled a couple out. She held them crumpled against her face and heaved noiseless sobs.

"It's okay, take it easy." Liz offered Diane a cigarette. "Do you think your friend could be right?" She fished through her purse for a lighter.

Diane's voice was muffled through the tissues. "Maybe. Michelle Gretson. She hates me."

Liz found her lighter and flicked it several times until the flame stood tall. Diane leaned over it, trying to light the cigarette, but she was crying too hard to inhale long enough. Liz took it from her, putting it between her own lips and inhaling until the tip of the cigarette glowed fiercely. She handed it back to Diane. "Who's Michelle?"

After a long drag on the cigarette, Diane said, "She and Ron were a thing for a while in high school." Her voice was almost calm as she looked across the room at the window. "I always thought she never got over him." She glanced at Liz and continued, "Michelle always tries to talk to him when we check out of the MiniMart. That's where she works. And I know," she continued, a shard of accusation in her voice, "I just *know* she waits to fill her car up until Ron's on duty. And then she's there all the time. She probably just rides around the block and then goes back for another dollar's worth of gas." Diane pressed more tissues to her face. The soft, curved moons of her upper cheeks were stained with cheap mascara.

Liz got up and went to the kitchen, returning with a glass ashtray that she set on the coffee table. "Don't jump to conclusions. It's probably nothing."

Diane stared absently in front of her, sliding the cigarette between her thumb and index finger. She sniffled loudly and inhaled slowly, coughing as she exhaled smoke.

"You're probably getting yourself all worked up for nothing," Liz said.

Diane turned her face to look at Liz, her eyebrows lifted in a hopeful arch. "Maybe you're right." She blinked and one final tear traveled the side of her face and absorbed into her hair. "Amber will be up from her nap. I better go." Diane set her drink on the coffee table and put her cigarette out with one quick stab in the ashtray. She stood, her fingers swiping against her damp cheeks.

"Keep me posted, Diane. And don't worry." Liz walked her to the door. "Come up any time, any time you feel like talking."

"Thanks."

Liz stepped forward and put her arms awkwardly around Diane's shoulders. It was a brief moment and Liz wondered how they looked, how someone would describe them if they saw them huddled for that second on the dirty linoleum. Did they look like friends? "Don't worry," she said again, her voice more forceful.

Diane seemed slightly embarrassed by the embrace and stepped back clumsily, her foot kicking the wall. She turned the doorknob and looked back at Liz. "You're right. I'm probably just imagining things." Liz listened as Diane's footsteps echoed on the wooden stairs.

That evening, Liz stood by her bedroom window watching for Ron to park his truck in the driveway. The glass was dirty, probably hadn't been washed in years. As cars passed on the street below, she began to shiver. Finally, she climbed into bed, gathering the covers around her. She tried to sleep, but she couldn't relax. After several hours, she finally drifted into a fitful sleep, her eyes opening when the first light splayed across the ceiling. Immediately she scrambled to the window, drawing a deep sigh of relief at the sight of Ron's truck in the driveway.

✿   ✿   ✿

In late March, Liz noticed the tiny purple crocuses ringing the large tree in the front yard. She'd survived the winter. The following week, the college was on spring break and Liz went to Chicago to interview at a private high school. She stayed an extra day to look at apartments and realized she'd have to work a second job to afford rent for even a studio. She guessed that meant a retail job of some kind, nights and weekends selling clothes or books. Or maybe she'd waitress. No, she wouldn't do that. That was absurd. She had a doctorate. She'd negotiate with the headmaster for an increased salary when he made the offer. A week later, she got the form letter that began, "Thank you for your interest . . . ." She couldn't believe it. She had interviewed well. She'd left the school knowing she was a shoe-in. She called the headmaster who told her in a quiet, tired voice, "We had an unusual number of very qualified applicants."

"But I have a PhD," Liz interjected, "and I've taught on the university level."

"Yes, that's true of many of the candidates, including the one we hired," he said in the same weary tone. Liz sensed that he'd said this at least a few times, that she wasn't the only shocked person who had called him. She mumbled thank you and heard him tell her good luck as she was hanging up.

I'm trapped, she thought, *trapped*, as she sobbed. I can't stay here. No way can I stay here. She considered going back to school for something else. An MBA. That would mean taking out a loan and living in a graduate dorm. Her current apartment, although in Indiana, was roomy and private. Living in a cramped dorm room, a shared restroom down the hall? She just couldn't. One morning, though, while sitting in her office, she phoned a few schools in Chicago only to learn that she'd missed the application deadlines. "Damn last straw," she said to no one. She stood and gathered up her purse. I need some fresh air, she thought.

She heard a knock on the door and opened it. When she saw it was Zach Millner, the dean of the college, she opened the door more widely.

"Headed out?" he asked, eyeing the purse over her shoulder.

"No. Well, I was, but I'm in no rush. Come in."

Zach, robust and in his fifties, sat on the only other free chair in her small office. "Your evaluations are the best in the French department."

Liz laughed. "Zach, there's only two of us in the department."

Removing his glasses to polish the lenses with his handkerchief, he said, "Frankly, they're the best in the college." He looked at Liz. "So, what do we need to do to keep you around here?"

Liz swallowed and said, "I don't know."

"Of course, there'll be a raise. It was going to be the standard ten percent, but I'm prepared to go to the trustees and say that in your case it should be fifteen."

"Thank you."

"So you're staying?"

She drew in a breath and said, "I haven't decided yet. I'd really like to get back to Chicago."

Zach sighed loudly and shook his head. "We lose so many of you young people to Chicago. The college isn't going to survive if we can't hang on to a few of you." He tapped his hands lightly on his thighs. "Hear me out. I'm going on sabbatical next year. My wife and I are looking for a housesitter. So, you could live there rent-free." He tilted his head, looking suddenly boyish, and smiled briefly. "With all the money you'd save, you could travel to Chicago, or anywhere, a lot."

One more year. Just one. Liz nodded. "That's true."

Zach jumped to his feet. "Excellent. My secretary will get the contract over to you this afternoon." Liz sensed he left quickly because he knew she hadn't actually agreed to stay.

I don't have to sign the contract, I can still leave, she told herself. She picked up her purse again and left her office.

Walking out of the building, she brushed shoulders with a student who stopped and said, "Oh, 'scuse me." Liz started to respond when she realized it was Ron.

"What are you doing here?"

He looked at her for a moment, then shrugged his shoulders and turned his head. "It's pretty here. Sometimes I come over on my lunch hour and walk around."

"I've never seen you here before."

"Well, I don't come in the winter." His hand rested flat against his stomach. "You got an office or something?"

Nodding, she said, "I do. You know, I bet Diane would love to have lunch with you. Amber too."

His gaze became direct, his eyes at a full stop. "You think so?"

Liz didn't answer. Ron turned and walked across the lawn, blending in so easily with the students although he carried no books. He turned into the narrow alley behind the library and then he was gone. Everything was gone. Her job at DePaul, Michael, Chicago, her life.

She began to walk, retracing his steps until she found him leaning against the back of the building, a cigarette in his hand. He showed no surprise but stretched his arm to offer her the cigarette.

Months later, she asked herself why she took it. Why hadn't she turned around, walked back to her office and locked the door? If she had, she wouldn't be sitting here now in her car in a parking lot, gripping the steering wheel as if she were driving through heavy traffic.

"Can you see anything?" Diane asked from the back seat.

"Not yet. Stay down." Shivering, Liz crossed her arms and slid her hands into the sleeves of her bulky sweater. Autumn had come early.

"Do you see Ron's truck? There's another one in town just like it but Ron's license plate starts with a B."

"No, it's not here. I told you, Diane, this is all in your mind. What time did you say she gets off from work?"

"Six. But sometimes, she works later."

Squinting, Liz tried to see beyond the glass door of the grocery store.

"Liz?"

"Yeah?"

"Promise me something, okay?"

"What?"

"Promise me you won't move back to Chicago, okay? You're the only person I can talk to about Ron. Liz?"

"*Shhh!*"

"Why? No one can hear us. Promise me you'll stay."

The MiniMart door swung open and a young woman in faded jeans walked out. She bounced a little when she walked, stepping all the way up to her toes before putting the next foot down. Her wavy auburn hair all but covered her red and white cashier's smock. A wave of jealousy jack-knifed through Liz. If the car had been running, she might've stepped on the gas.

"Liz? Promise me. Don't leave."

She watched the woman get into her own car, an old Volkswagen. After watching the car roll backwards and then out of the lot, Liz finally answered Diane, "I'm not going anywhere."

MARCASITE

Brenda felt old-fashioned. She ordinarily wore pierced earrings, but today she wore her grandmother's clip-on marcasite and pearl earrings. She found the dusky, quiet sheen of marcasite so much prettier than flashy, contemporary jewelry. The earrings, with their tiny stones gleaming softly like a cluster of petite stars set against a silver night, were mysterious to her.

The earrings were reserved for special occasions. Presented to her on her sixteenth birthday, Brenda had worn them on every birthday since, on the day of her college graduation, and, of course, on her wedding day in fulfillment of the "something old" requirement. Today was not yet auspicious, but she hoped that the earrings would bring her and her husband, Dave, good luck. They were going to look at a house for sale. They had looked at several already but this morning Brenda had awoken with a strong feeling of anticipation, a certainty that this would be *the* house. She wore the earrings as a positive portent, insurance that her instinct wasn't misguided.

She peered at her reflection in the bathroom mirror and adjusted the left earring so that the pearl dangle hung straight. She applied only a little make-up, a dab of blush on her cheeks and almost imperceptible lipstick. It was a warm day, so she gathered her long brown hair up into a bun. I look almost like Grandmother, she thought, smiling. She heard Dave call to her that it was time to go. Still staring at herself in the mirror, Brenda reached her arm to turn off the light. There was a slight buzzing as the fluorescent light flickered on and off for a few seconds, Brenda's face appearing and disappearing in the glass, before it extinguished completely and the room was dark and quiet. Brenda quickly picked up her purse and went to join Dave.

They'd been married for one year, the Mathisons, a first marriage for both of them although they were in their thirties. Dave taught economics at Decorah College and Brenda was chief researcher at the Decorah Historical Society. Almost everything in the small town was named Decorah something or other.

Before their wedding, Brenda and Dave lived on opposite sides of the little park that separated the east and west sides of town. Brenda often stayed the night at Dave's apartment and walked home early in the morning, when the town was still quiet, taking one of the many brick paths that crossed the park. Their love affair was new, so fresh. She felt exhilarated on those mornings, a euphoria lodged in the center of her chest. After the wedding, Brenda boxed up her things and moved into Dave's apartment. From time to time, she would walk across the park by herself and look at the apartment building she used to live in. She gazed up at the unfamiliar ivory-colored curtains hanging in the windows of the apartment on the second floor, and noticed the small blue Toyota parked in her old spot in the driveway. My old life, she caught herself thinking once.

Dave's apartment was small and cramped. They couldn't wait to move. Like many people in Decorah, they hoped for a house on the east side of town where large older homes lined wide streets with enormous trees, survivors of the Dutch elm disease that had devastated much of the area in the thirties and forties. Many of the houses were in need of considerable repair, but owners and admirers agreed that older homes had character that just couldn't be found in the newer homes located in the outer subdivisions of town.

Brenda had always wanted to live in a big old house, a house that didn't open up to you as soon as you stepped through the door, that let you see the living and dining rooms from the foyer. No, she wanted a house with many rooms, each with a different mood, self-sufficient, not dependent on the rest of the house but contributing to its overall character. She wanted to sit in a room, absorb and appreciate its substance before moving on to another room to do the same. Houses, like life, took time. There was no need to rush.

❦   ❦   ❦

As they drove past the park, Brenda placed her left hand on Dave's thigh, kneading the soft material of his khaki slacks between her fingers. She looked at Dave's profile and could see that he was happy, humming along to whatever song was on the radio that Brenda didn't recognize. His jaw was lifted a bit as he peered over the steering wheel at the gray pavement.

Despite her earlier optimism, Brenda was nervous about seeing the house. Few people in Decorah used realtors; houses generally sold quickly by word-of-mouth advertising, and the Mathisons never even had a chance to bid on several houses. People selling houses often had several offers and would arbitrarily choose a buyer. It wasn't always the top bidder who got a house. The oldest generation in Decorah were famously picky about whom they deemed worthy successors to their homes.

As their car turned right on Chestnut Street, Brenda noticed how dark everything seemed. Despite the bright sun, the huge elm trees provided enough shade to make the sky seem overcast. She looked up straining to see the sun, but it was as if they were driving through a tunnel. The branches of the trees were covered with a green denseness extending out into the street and almost meeting their counterparts on the other side. It was a very quiet street, no bicycles or even people walking. As the house came into view, Dave pulled over to the curb and turned off the ignition.

Amanda Lewiston's house was on the corner of Chestnut and Pine Place. A large orange brick house with black shutters, it was in remarkably good condition, at least from the outside. Its high-pitched slate roof gave the house the appeal of a country home. The two upstairs front windows contained matching lead glass patterns. Squinting, Brenda looked at the front door, quarter-sawn oak, solid and heavy, and decorated with an in-laid panel of rose-colored glass. She knew from previous drives past the house that Dave admired the L-shaped porch that hugged the front and left sides of the house. There was a perfect spot for a porch swing. Brenda closed her eyes and could almost feel herself swaying.

The Mathisons had made inquiries and knew a bit about the owner. Amanda had lived alone for the last eight years, since her husband, John, had died. He had bought the house in his early thirties while still a bachelor, and brought his bride there a couple of years later. John had taught English at Decorah College, but his real passion had been the house. He spent considerable time researching its history and hunting for antique furniture of the best quality. A favorite faculty anecdote involved John's arriving late for a graduation ceremony because he was occupied with getting the screens up and had lost track of time. As he got older, John had refused to allow anyone to help him with the grounds and was often seen mowing the picturesque front yard or painting the shutters a glossy black. As he entered his eighties, the

Lewistons became fairly reclusive, although John's funeral was well attended.

Dave wiggled his eyebrows up and down as he smiled broadly. "Time to face the music?"

Brenda turned and gazed at the house. At once it seemed familiar, friendly. "Dave, this is it. I know we're going to buy this house. I feel it."

"I love you, my fortune teller."

Brenda stretched her arm to touch the side of his left cheek with her open palm and said, "Don't ever stop." Turning his face, he kissed her hand.

As they went up the stone walk, Brenda noticed the tiny white flowers planted on both sides. Ahead, a bank of cerulean forget-me-nots was planted close to the house behind a small wall of piled rocks that stood in front of the flowers and ran the length of the house.

"Honey, you'll have a lot of gardening to do," Brenda said.

"No, Bren," Dave laughed, "*you'll* have a lot of gardening to do."

"It's settled; we'll hire a gardener."

Dave rang the bell and they waited. After a minute, Dave was about to ring again when the oak door opened and a tiny figure appeared. Brenda could not make out the woman's features, but she spoke quickly, "You must be the Mathisons. I'm Amanda, please come in." She held the door and they entered, Brenda first.

"Thank you, I hope we're on time," Dave said.

Amanda didn't answer, but continued, "So, you're in the economics department at the College? Is Bud Granger still there? He and my husband got along famously. Oh, surely he's retired by now."

Dave started to speak a couple of times but stopped when it became clear that Amanda intended to ramble on. She mentioned teaching French at the college years ago when a member of that department took ill suddenly. For years she was involved with the Decorah College Women's Association but that organization had disbanded when some of the younger women objected to the formality of the spring and fall afternoon teas.

Brenda looked around but the house seemed darker than the street. She felt a bit chilly and wished she had worn a sweater. Amanda directed them to the parlor where they sat down on various chairs. Seated near a window, Amanda's face became clearly visible for the first time. The woman must have been near eighty years old but her eyes were remarkably blue, framed with long lashes. Brenda noticed the web of skinny blue and violet veins on her forehead. Amanda couldn't have been more than five feet and she was very thin. Everything about her, Brenda thought, seemed frail although her thick silver hair fell abundantly onto her shoulders. Admiring it, Brenda resolved not to cut her own hair when it grayed. Then she worried that her bun might look silly. Amanda wore a lavender sweater with a simple white linen skirt. Brenda spotted the gold band Amanda wore on her left ring finger over another ring set with a large emerald. Her husband selected her birthstone for her engagement ring, Brenda guessed, perhaps because her own birthday was in May. Or maybe the ring had belonged to John's mother or grandmother. Brenda reached up and felt her earrings to make sure the correct side of the pearl dangles was still facing front.

"The house was the first one on the block, you know," Amanda said. "The original owner ran the mill in Avon, just down the old highway. My husband verified the date as 1871. He was quite certain that it's the oldest home on Chestnut." Dave cleared his throat to say something but Amanda asked, "Brenda, you work at the Historical Society? How do you like it?"

"Oh, it's interesting. I get to do some challenging research." Brenda wondered if she should say more about her job, about the research she had done on Decorah, but she didn't want to appear a know-it-all and perhaps offend Amanda who seemed to know so much about the town herself.

"John found the people there very pleasant," Amanda said. "They undertook quite a lot of work for him. Now then, you probably would like to see the house." Amanda stood and ran her hands over the top of her hair. "Let's start with the kitchen."

As Brenda and Dave followed the tiny woman from room to room, Brenda realized that she couldn't concentrate. She looked at Dave. He was clearly absorbed by the charm of the house and asked questions. He opened the cherry cupboards in the kitchen and asked politely if he could run water from the brass faucets in the downstairs bathroom. He inquired about when the oak flooring was laid, the cost of utilities each month, the height of the ceilings, the efficiency of the fireplaces and more. They were the right questions. Brenda could tell that Amanda was impressed with Dave's attention to detail. When he mentioned, not so subtly, that his grandfather had been a master cabinetmaker who had learned his craft in Germany and had later sold his own furniture in upstate New York, Amanda's face lit up and Brenda knew the house was theirs. No matter who else looked at the house, Amanda would give Dave and Brenda first consideration.

Brenda, however, felt isolated from Amanda and Dave's increasingly friendly conversation. She found she was studying Amanda rather than the house, and she wanted to ask a different set of questions: What would she do after she sold the house? Where would she go? How could she part with the house? Was she terribly lonely since her husband had died?

"Brenda?" Dave said.

"Yes?" she blurted, realizing she sounded startled.

"Honey, Mrs. Lewiston asked you if you liked lace curtains."

"Oh, excuse me, I was so interested in the view from the window that I started to daydream. The curtains are lovely. They're perfect for the windows."

Brenda thought Dave looked concerned. He thinks I don't like the house, she thought, and tried to focus on their comments and look interested. Amanda announced that they would take the main stairwell up to the second floor and the back stairwell down again. Amanda proceeded up the stairs a step at time, grasping the banister while Brenda and Dave followed patiently behind. On the second floor, they entered a large bedroom done in pastel blues and greens. The room had an ethereal quality; it almost seemed to float. Sunlight flooded through the windows and reflected off the bureau's mirrors. The glass in the windows was quite old, Brenda noted, thicker at the base from years of gravity causing it to flow downwards. The glass above the base shimmered as if you were looking through water, everything behind it a drowned image. After walking through the dark house, the light was so unexpected that they were all silent a moment. Amanda finally said, "And this is the master bedroom." She began to walk about the room, to point out the crown molding, a small flash leaping from her hand. The emerald, Brenda realized, and she stared at it, followed its gleam in Amanda's every movement. Light burned the stone until it became a small, green flame. Then Amanda slipped her hand in the pocket of her skirt and the flame died.

Brenda felt dizzy suddenly, the room starting to sweep about her, and for a moment she thought she might faint. She had an image of herself lying on the pale blue carpet while Dave and Amanda stood over her, their figures blocking the sunlight. But then she heard Amanda's voice, something about the light from the southern exposure, and she felt herself again. She walked with Dave to join Amanda at the large window that extended from the ceiling almost to the floor. They looked down at the back yard, a seemingly endless lawn punctuated every now and then by stone garden sculptures and beds of flowers. It looks like a cemetery, Brenda thought, startling herself.

The rest of the tour was a blur. Later, when Brenda tried to recall the house, she had vague images of lace curtains hanging in tall, narrow windows and lots of heavy, dark furniture. She remembered a few large closets but couldn't place them in the house. Did the kitchen have a pantry? How many bedrooms were there? Brenda tried to picture the library but found she couldn't. What she did remember was the musty smell pervading the house and her longing to open the windows and let in fresh air. The sense of the past was overwhelming, stifling. It was present in the family china and crystal, the framed photos resting on bureaus and desks, the tablecloths embroidered with the letter "L" in a delicate script. Everything was generations old. Brenda was relieved when she finally heard Dave tell Amanda that they'd be leaving, but would be in touch soon.

As they settled themselves into the car, Dave said, "Hon, you were so strange. You seemed so out of it."

"I didn't mean to be. Sorry."

"What's the problem? We finally find a gem of a house and it was like you were sleepwalking."

Yes, that was how she felt. Dave knew her so well. Looking down at her hands, she began to twirl her wedding band around her finger. "I'm worried about Amanda," she said quietly. She snatched a tissue out of the box on the dashboard and pressed it to her forehead, blotting the tiny beads of moisture. "I'm worried about Amanda and I'm worried about me."

"You? Why are you worried about you?"

She looked through the windshield and tried to find light through the tree branches. "I'm worried about being old and alone in a house that's going to outlive you, me, and whoever lives there after us."

Dave laughed, reaching over to playfully tap the end of her nose. "Is that all?"

Pressing her back against the seat, Brenda said, "I'm serious. There's something about the house that's spooking me. Like it will make us old before our time. I don't know. It just made me feel strange."

Dave began to tap the tips of his fingers against the steering wheel. "The house is perfect," she said, "and I know she's going to sell it to us. I just don't know if we're ready, that's all."

"Ready for what?"

"Ready to not be young any more." That was it. Brenda felt she had aged at least a generation in one afternoon.

Dave touched his fists to his forehead in mock exasperation. "Buying a house doesn't make you old. A mortgage doesn't make you ready for AARP."

A long sliver of light penetrated the windshield and Brenda saw the street clearly. Despite the warmth, she shivered, a chill moving through her. Rubbing her hands over her forearms, she told her husband, "You're right. It's the best house we've seen We should buy it."

"Yes!" Dave raised his arm, his hand clenched triumphantly. He turned the car on and edged away from the curb.

Brenda pulled down the sun visor and caught sight of her face in the mirror located on the back of the flap. Her bun had slipped a bit and strands of her hair hung loose about her face. As she smoothed the wisps behind her ears, she realized with a start that her right earring was missing. She quickly ran her hands over the folds of her skirt and looked at the floor in the car. I must've lost it in the house, she thought. Looking at herself in the mirror, she removed the left earring. As she did, she noticed the tiny lines at the corners of her eyes. They spread in perfect symmetry to form a fan reaching for each temple. She turned to tell Dave about the missing earring, but then decided against telling him. I'll call Amanda when I get home.

But she didn't. Dave called Amanda to discuss the price and turned to Brenda, waving a jubilant thumbs up. Brenda could have easily asked Dave to give her the phone for a moment, but she couldn't bring herself to do so. Instead, while he was still on the phone, she jotted a note and waved it in front of him. "Walking to store," it said.

The air was soft but not muggy and Brenda breathed deeply. Approaching the park, she stopped to look at the flowerbeds, clusters of red and yellow flowers clinging together like miniature people in a crowd. Instead of going directly to the store, she detoured and went to look at the apartment building she used to live in.

Standing at the edge of the driveway, she watched as two young women emerged from the side door, Brenda's former entrance. The women were in their early to mid-twenties, she guessed. Did they share the apartment? As they walked down the driveway, Brenda noticed their clothes, gym shorts and T-shirts. They both had dark blonde hair pulled up into disheveled ponytails. As they reached the sidewalk, Brenda started to walk behind them as though she were simply walking down the block. After a few steps, the girls each put on a headset and began jogging, their ponytails moving back and forth in an identical swing. I can't keep up with them, Brenda thought. Even when they were just formless shapes far ahead of her, she tried not to lose sight of them.

DUST

The receptionist hung up the phone and it rang again immediately. "Allergies and audiology," she said, holding the phone between her head and her shoulder while her fingers tapped the keyboard in front of her.

Rachel Harris, sitting in the waiting room where she had a view of the receptionist in the wood-paneled and glass booth, had been listening to this refrain, "allergies and audiology," since she began coming to this clinic for shots these last few years. Looking around the waiting room, Rachel could easily discern who was allergy and who was audiology. Patients were either sniffling into tissues or shouting something, often, "My hearing aid isn't working!" at the receptionist or a fellow patient.

She often wondered why the clinic coupled allergies with audiology. The only thing she could come up with was the alphabetical sequence, the alliteration. Were pediatrics and podiatry housed together on another floor?

She looked at two posters side by side on the wall directly across from the receptionist's booth. The first one was a colorful sketch of a small boy with yellow hair smiling as he held big white pillows on either side of his head over his ears. The caption read, "Start Protecting Your Hearing Now." People normally averted their eyes from the second poster, a hugely magnified drawing of a dust mite. This caption read, "Invisible to the Naked Eye." Flinching as she looked at the spidery, humped bug, Rachel wondered why *everyone* wasn't allergic to dust mites, why everyone's immune system radar didn't perk up to their presence and say, *no way*. She felt an odd pride that her body was aware enough to put up a defense against something so repulsive, but she worried her allergies would worsen, that she'd become asthmatic like Rose Braxton, the girl in her third grade class who'd died from a respiratory disorder.

Rachel thought of Rose every year on Ash Wednesday. She had a memory of them standing in line together at church when they were very little, both of them frightened to approach the altar. The priest dipped his thumb into a small brass urn of ashes before he made a heavy black cross on their foreheads. Rachel had trembled as she felt the charred particles scratch her skin, the priest telling her in a voice tired from repetition, "Remember, man, that you are dust and unto dust you shall return." Dust and death, the two were forever linked in her mind. And then Rose died, the first death Rachel had ever experienced. The empty desk in the classroom jolted her whenever she dared turn her head to look. When Rachel was first diagnosed, at twenty-two, as being allergic to dust, she had thought, *I'm allergic to death*. It struck her as logical. Shouldn't everyone be allergic to death?

"Rachel Harris," a nurse called.

Rachel stood and walked into the injection office. The nurse who normally gave Rachel her injections, Tina, must have been on vacation. Tina would have asked her right away how she was holding up as a new single mother, aware that Rachel's husband, Ted, had moved out the previous month. This nurse, whose name tag said "Ginny," didn't bother with chit chat, but instead immediately pressed the tiny needle into the fleshy outer-side of Rachel's upper arm. Rachel inhaled until she felt a tug at the bottom of her lungs and then exhaled slowly, trying to relax. She looked at the numerous tiny glass bottles filled with serum resting on what looked like a small kitchen counter. People were allergic to so many different things: dust, grass, trees, ragweed, mold. Allergens were everywhere, waiting to congest sinuses and make eyes water.

Rachel was usually calm when Tina administered the shots. Tina was just a few years older than Rachel, somewhere in her late twenties. She was very skinny, always talking a blue streak. Tina didn't suffer from allergies herself, but the end of her nose was always red and she clutched a balled tissue in one of her hands at all times. Her voice had a nasal coating and Rachel couldn't always discern the endings of her words. Tina, also a single mother, told Rachel that her little boy came home from day care with every cold that was being passed around, and she usually caught it as well.

Once, soon after she began getting injections, Rachel had walked back into the reception area to wait the thirty minutes required to make sure she wasn't having a reaction to the shot when she felt a growing itch in her vagina travel down her thighs. Embarrassed, she thought her khakis were too tight, that they were irritating her crotch. Her face began to feel hot and she realized, oh, *this* was a reaction. She told the receptionist who jumped to her feet and ushered Rachel into the injection office. Tina ran for the doctor, a tall gray-haired man with thick glasses, who quickly tied a rubber tourniquet around Rachel's upper arm and, while she looked away, pushed a needle into the hollow of her elbow, injecting her with something to stop the reaction. He gave her Seldane tablets and told her she would have to wait at least an hour in the waiting room before going home so they could be sure the reaction had been thoroughly checked.

Rachel had been at the edge of a screaming panic throughout the several moments from when she first became aware of the reaction until the doctor untied the tourniquet. Then she was flooded with all kinds of sensations: fear, relief, fatigue. She knew that people could die from such overdoses of allergens. The doctor asked her how she first knew she was having a reaction. Blushing, she told him about the itch in her vagina, and he looked back at her blankly. Rachel thought she had given a ridiculous answer, she felt mortified, but then she noticed Tina standing behind the doctor, nodding at her, encouraging her to keep speaking and tell the doctor everything. When he left the room, Tina told her, "Reactions often begin in a mucous membrane. Female patients sometimes first detect the sensation in their vaginas. No need to be embarrassed. None at all." She told Rachel that they would lower the dosage of the shot and then increase it more gradually over the next few months.

After that, Rachel was on her guard. A few times, after getting an injection, she had left the waiting room and walked back into the injection office and said to Tina, "I think I'm having a reaction." Tina would look at her, at her face, and shake her head no.

"I don't think so, but I'll get the doctor if you want me too."

Rachel would stammer, "I guess I'm all right. I just felt a little funny. I thought . . ."

Tina would smile. "It's normal. After you have a reaction, you think every body sensation is the start of something. Believe me, you'll know if it happens."

Her reassurance made Rachel feel safe. This new nurse, however, didn't know her, and Rachel worried that if she stepped back in the office and told her she thought she was having a reaction, the nurse would simply run and get the doctor. Then she'd have to face the tourniquet and needle again or the doctor's irritation at being called in for a false alarm. Rachel walked back into the reception room and told herself that she could get through the thirty minutes without incident. She had learned that the best thing to do was distract herself. Read. Eavesdrop on the other patients' conversations. Balance her checkbook. If she didn't have a reaction the first few minutes, she told herself, she was probably safe.

Rachel and Ted had been married for four years. They had met when she was a freshman at Loyola and Ted a senior. After dating throughout Rachel's college years, they married the Saturday after her graduation. Two years later, when Rachel was twenty-three, she and Ted had a son, Craig, now two. Last month, Ted told Rachel he wanted to marry one of his clients, Beverly, a wealthy woman with no children and two Alaskan huskies. Ted had met her when he prepared her taxes and his explanation to Rachel was, "She's my soulmate."

Sitting in the reception room, Rachel wished for the umpteenth time that she hadn't married so young, that she should have gotten at least a master's degree before agreeing to marriage. As she resisted the urge to scratch her arm, she thought wryly that she should have made herself wait for at least thirty minutes before answering yes or no to Ted's proposal. Wasn't it obvious, she thought now, that they were allergic to each other?

Getting injected with gradually increasing amounts of dust and dust mites was supposed to help Rachel stop sneezing when she vacuumed the carpet or polished the furniture. Marriage should have been like that, she thought. She and Ted should have only exposed themselves to each other in small doses, built up a tolerance for each other, before deciding to spend the rest of their lives together. They had lived and fought in their cramped, no longer cute, apartment and it was no surprise, Rachel realized now, that they had a negative reaction to each other. At least dust mites are invisible, she thought now; I should have seen Ted a mile off.

Finding out about Beverly had been jarring, though. The soulmate comment made her wretch. Thinking about Ted walking those Alaskan huskies, throwing a stick and both of those masses of bushy white fur running to retrieve it, had been too much. She imagined this faceless Beverly sliding an arm around Ted's waist as they waited for the dogs to return so they could pet them and say "Good boys!" Rachel had looked about their apartment and the thought of being left there with a two year old who didn't sleep through the night seemed outrageously unfair. Picturing herself working at the local K-Mart for minimum wage to make ends meet, most of her earnings going to their regular baby-sitter, made her temper explode. She had picked up her bowl of cereal and thrown it on the floor, screaming, "You bastard! You absolute bastard!" Thirty minutes, she thought now. All I needed was thirty minutes and I could have kept my cool.

The door to the waiting room opened. The newest patient took his time closing it and the winter air gusted through the room. He looked to be in his mid-thirties, with long legs as thin as matchsticks cased in black denim jeans. An aerial view of the earth was on the front of his black T-shirt, the words, "The Grateful Dead - Endless World Tour," written above and below the globe. Rachel looked at him and guessed allergies but she was wrong. He hollered something at the receptionist about having missed his appointment earlier in the day and not knowing the phone number to call and explain why. The receptionist smiled at him as if he were a charming, mischievous child.

"Are you still working with the amplifiers?" she called out to him through the small, circular opening in the glass.

"What?" he yelled back.

"Are you still doing sound for that rock band?" She almost matched the volume of his voice.

He understood, nodding his head, and the receptionist shook a reprimanding finger at him. He laughed and adjusted his hearing aid, a small, high-pitched whistle singing out into the quiet of the room. He re-scheduled the appointment and started to walk to the door.

Rachel felt a strange affinity with the man, following him with her eyes until he was out of sight, and she knew why. Almost three years ago, she and Ted went to Cincinnati when she was pregnant with Craig to attend a family reunion. They had stayed at a Holiday Inn for three nights. Each morning as she left the lobby of the hotel, Rachel noticed men and women in their late teens and early twenties dressed almost identically in navy blue suits and crisp white shirts. Occasionally, she saw a woman with a quietly-colored scarf added to her outfit for flair, but the accessory didn't ease the severity of the corporate uniform. The men wore black shoes that tied and the women wore low, navy pumps. She asked the desk clerk, a young man with a ponytail and a gold stud earring, what group they were with and he answered, "Oh, they're the Young Republicans. They come every year." He started to roll his eyes but then stopped, glancing at Rachel's own casual outfit. It must've passed his test because he continued, "They're a real pain in the ass."

Laughing lightly, Rachel said, "Oh?"

He nodded. "They don't care about wasting water. They make the maids change the sheets every day and they ask for more soap and shampoo and then they pack it in their suitcases when they leave. They never leave tips but they fill out the survey cards and tell us everything we do wrong."

On the morning of their last day in Cincinnati, Rachel looked out the window to see if it was raining and noticed the campers and trailers in the open lot across the street. People in tie-dye shirts and bright bandannas on their heads were walking about or sitting on the ground on blankets. Even with the window shut, Rachel could hear music. A couple of guys were painting a huge poster in psychedelic swirls of purple and fuschia, that said, "The Dead Live." Rachel wrinkled her forehead and then said, "Oh! The Grateful Dead are in town."

By the time she and Ted got down to the lobby, she noticed people coming in the door with umbrellas; the rain had started. Ted went to the desk to check out while Rachel sat in a chair to wait. The Young Republicans started to emerge from the elevator and enter the lobby, each of them carrying a plain navy or black umbrella. With no warning, lightning bounced through the large picture window and everyone prepared themselves for the clap of thunder but they were still jolted by how loudly it sounded and the way the building shook. No one wanted to leave the hotel in the downpour, so people stood in the crowded lobby, talking and guessing about when the rain might let up.

The door opened and a steady stream of wet Deadheads ran into the lobby. Rachel was struck by their hair, so much of it, lying over their backs in ponytails, braids, or pouring in an avalanche over shoulders and chests. There were children too, excited by the dash across the street in the rain and into the hotel. Rachel stood amidst the throng of people and felt happy, buoyed up by the camaraderie that comes when a group of people, in safe surroundings, watches something dangerous together. More lightning flashed and the thunder was directly overhead, crashing and pounding. People were quiet for a moment after the thunder sounded and then exclaimed whether that crash had been louder than the previous one. A man with a long gray beard exclaimed, "Goodness, gracious, great balls-o-fire!" and Rachel laughed out loud.

Glancing about, she realized that the Young Republicans didn't share in the merriment. They looked at each other, widening their eyes and stretching their mouths into ridiculing smirks. Rachel overheard one woman in a blue suit say to another, "Get them *out* of here." The Deadheads seemed to sense their attitude and soon the lobby was divided into two camps, the Young Republicans retreating in single file against the back wall while the casual crowd sat on the floor and lounged up against one another. The room grew ominously quiet when the man with the long gray beard approached the line of blue suits and slapped his hand on the shoulder of a man with very short red hair. "Here for the concert, friend?" the Deadhead bellowed. Rachel laughed again but her sound was lost under the next burst of thunder.

Many of the blue-suited people looked at the desk clerk to see if he would assume some command and usher the concert goers out of the lobby. The young man Rachel had spoken to, however, came from behind the desk and started talking with a group of women in ankle-length skirts about some terrific bootleg Dead tapes he had gotten in Buffalo. One of the women exclaimed, "The Dead *love* Buffalo! Great people. Great concert town."

The lightning ceased and the thunder moved. Rachel could hear it in the distance now, fading rapidly. One by one, the Young Republicans made their way to the door, stopping to raise their umbrellas before running out into the rain. Rachel watched as each dark blue form ran into the parking lot and thought, it's not true; opposites don't attract. They react.

"These people need a bath," someone said into her ear. Turning, she wasn't surprised to find Ted, tucking a hotel receipt into his wallet.

"C'mon, it's fun." Rachel held up two fingers and said, "Peace."

"I'll bring the car around and you can run out."

She watched Ted walk through the lobby, pausing a moment before he ran into the rain. She raised her arms, lifting the back of her sweater over her head, and started to make her way to the door. Impulsively, she stopped to talk to a man in a jean jacket, the arms ripped off, who looked about her age.

"Why are they called 'The Grateful Dead'?"

The man smiled broadly, eager to explain, and Rachel saw he was missing one of his front teeth.

"If you're grateful to be dead, you don't expect anything out of life. No disappointments. Anything that happens is okay, it's cool."

"Okay," Rachel said.

"Life is a gamble. Nothing is safe. You may as well be dead. Accept it. Be glad. Be grateful."

Concerned he would never stop, Rachel said, "Thank you. I think I've got it."

"Say, you want to hang out with us before the show?"

Rachel smiled and shook her head no. "I wish I could, but I'm leaving town."

"Truckin, huh? That's good. You got to keep on moving or you die. You sit around waiting for anything and you die. But see, we're already dead. He tapped his fingers on his chest and said, "We don't care, you know? We're already there."

He continued speaking as Rachel held up her hand and waved good-bye to him.

🪷　　　🪷　　　🪷

In the waiting room, Rachel's upper arm erupted with prickly heat and she fought the urge to scratch it. It's normal, she told herself, perfectly normal. Stay calm. But she couldn't. She imagined a small, intense fire raging and spreading deep within her arm. She crossed her legs and then wished she hadn't, the fabric of her jeans moving in a way to make her think a vaginal reaction was on the way. Fumbling, she opened her purse, hunting through it to find her checkbook so she could distract herself with arithmetic. Taking out her pen, she heard giggles from the corner of the waiting room.

Turning her head, Rachel looked at the two girls. She recognized one of them, the husky girl with light brown hair who had been getting shots the same time as Rachel for at least a year or so. She knew that the girl's name was Hannah, having heard the nurse call her into the injection office many times. Rachel guessed that Hannah and her friend were probably twelve or thirteen, but they tried to look older. Hannah wore overpowering blue eyeshadow that made the irises of her eyes look almost colorless in comparison. Pink lipstick, applied with a rookie's hand, rimmed the skin below her lower lip. The other girl had very dark, shoulder-length hair, brown eyes, and ample lips. Her eyebrows were as dark as her hair, arching into porticos above her eyes. Her dark outlinings were set dramatically against her thick, white complexion. She wore red lip-stick and a hint of red blush, but she wore it artfully, and the color suited her. Rachel listened to their conversation for a moment and learned that this girl's name was Erin.

The girls were laughing over a piece of paper resting on Erin's lap. Erin held a pencil over it, and said, "Okay, okay. Now I'll do you. Name three boys you'd like to marry."

"Let's see. Jason, for sure, and Kevin, and . . . oh, I don't know, I'll say Andy."

Erin made notations on the paper. "Now tell me three occupations you'd like your husband to be."

"That's easy," Hannah said. "A doctor, a lawyer, and an accountant."

"Why an accountant?" Erin asked.

Rachel shifted in her chair, leaning out over the arm rest, so she could hear the answer.

"Because they make money," Hannah answered matter-of-factly. "Isn't that what they do? Count money?"

Erin continued to interview Hannah, asking her to name three cities she wanted to live in, three cars she wanted to drive, three girls' names, three boys' names, the list went on and on. Her last question was, "Name three things you want to be?"

"What do you mean?" Hannah asked.

"You know," Erin said impatiently, "three things you want to be when you grow up, three occupations."

"Oh." Hannah crossed her legs, holding the sneaker on the raised leg in her hand. "I want to be . . . let's see . . .oh! I want to be a model, an actress, and nothing, a housewife, I mean."

The two girls leaned in so their heads touched each other. Erin was clearly doing some type of mathematical calculations as she tapped her pencil up and down the list, occasionally stopping to make a notation. Seeing this, Rachel was reminded that she meant to balance her checkbook, but she continued to watch the girls. They were a good distraction. Erin started to read the paper, but Hannah grabbed it from her.

"No, let me," Hannah said. "Okay. I'm going to marry Kevin. Darn! I wanted to marry Jason. And Kevin will be a lawyer, well, that's pretty good. We're going to live in Paris and have a daughter named Danielle and a son named Jason."

As Hannah said this, both girls burst out laughing. Hannah slapped her thigh, and said, "Kevin might object to naming our son after someone I used to be in love with."

"Ya think?!"

Hannah raised the paper and began to read again. "We'll drive a Porsche, live in an apartment. Shoot. I wanted it to be a mansion. We'll have a pet giraffe . . ."

They looked at each other in silence for a split second and again laughed hard.

"Well, I didn't know what to say after dog or cat," Hannah explained.

"I'm going to ask Kevin if he'll like living with a giraffe," Erin teased.

"Don't you dare! I'll kill you! I'll kill you!" Hannah's voice bubbled with pretend fear.

Erin hid her head in the nook of her elbow, calling out, "You better be nice to me or I'm going to *tee-ll!*"

Hannah leaned over, almost shouting into Erin's ear, and said, "If you *do,* I'll tell Christopher Janson you want to marry him!"

Now they both hid their heads, their upper bodies shaking with gleeful embarrassment.

"Wait," Hannah lifted her head. "I'm not done." She unfolded the paper which had gotten crinkled like a used tissue and said, "When I grow up, I'm going to be . . . *nothing!* All right!"

The nurse poked her head back in the room and said, "Rachel."

Rachel stood and walked back into the injection office. She had done it, gone thirty minutes without convincing herself she was having a reaction to the shot. She rolled up the sleeve of her turtleneck so the nurse could examine her arm. She felt the nurse's finger make a circular tracing on her skin.

"You have a wheel the size of a dime. Not bad."

Tina also noted reactions in this way, comparing the redness to the size of coins. Rachel waited while the nurse opened a tiny tube of cream and rubbed it over the puncture in her skin.

Smiling, the nurse said, "See you in a week."

"Thank you." Rachel took a step towards the door and then stopped. "Is Tina on vacation?"

"Tina?" The nurse looked at Rachel as if she hadn't heard her. "No. You don't know? Not vacation."

The nurse's voice wasn't irritated but there was something odd about it. "Is she sick? She always has a cold."

The nurse shook her head no, her neck barely moving. Her whisper was low, but hoarse. "She died. On Wednesday."

"What? What did you say?" Rachel's voice bellowed, filling the tiny examining room.

The nurse tried to take Rachel's hand. "I know, I know," she said, her other arm reaching to push the door shut. "It's a terrible shock. No one here can believe it."

Rachel felt a pulsing beneath her feet, as if the ground had a heartbeat. "Did you say she died? Is that what you said?"

The nurse nodded, watching Rachel with a clinical eye, checking for signs of physical distress.

"How?" Rachel realized now that she was shouting. She felt dizzy. Was the light over her head swinging? The nurse looked concerned and Rachel willed herself to lower her voice, asking, "How?"

"Heroin," the nurse answered quickly, softly, expecting Rachel's disbelief. "We were all shocked."

Rachel heard herself exhale. The nurse said more words. She was asking her if she needed a glass of water or did she want to sit down?

Rachel shook her head and walked out of the office. She was supposed to stop at the receptionist's booth and schedule her next injection but she walked past it and headed toward the door. She heard laughter chime through the room and she stopped abruptly in front of Hannah and Erin.

"*You*," she said, pointing a mean finger at Hannah "You are *not nothing!*" Rachel waved her finger with her words and felt short of breath. "You will be someday, we *all* will be someday, but today, right now, you are *not nothing!*"

She opened the door and stepped onto the sidewalk beyond. The glass door closed with a heavy, sucking noise, but she could still hear the girls' startled laughter as she walked away to the parking lot. And she could still hear phantom laughter in her ears as she drove away, finding her way to a main avenue, pushing her foot down on the gas. She told herself, I'll be fine, as long as I keep moving, as long as I stay distracted.

BEFORE DINNER

Cindy Dyson leaned over the bathroom sink, the heels of her feet lifted slightly from the floor tiles. Her skin was flushed from the hot shower and her head felt pleasantly light. She brushed her teeth and gargled with mouthwash. Smiling at her reflection in the glass, she felt something, a glimmer of happiness, or maybe just hope. She smoothed moisturizer around her eyes, watching it disappear but somehow, miraculously, plump the tiny wrinkles until they almost disappeared. Finally, she put on deodorant, rolling the wet ball under the hollow crescent of her arm. Cindy did all of this with the brisk efficiency of a person who has lived for years with children underfoot. Tonight, however, the children were downstairs finishing their dinners with Jennifer, the babysitter.

Her wedding and engagement rings sat next to her watch on the back of the sink. She pushed the rings onto her left ring finger, adjusting the diamond so it stood front and center. It was ten minutes before six o'clock. Mike had promised to be home by seven, not a minute later. Cindy imagined the argument they would have if he were late. It would be an easy argument to win, and she loved to win, but she reminded herself not to start it, not tonight. It would be better, much better, if she were gracious when Mike rushed in.

She heard noise coming from the kitchen below, the start of another fight between her small sons, and decided not to intervene. The babysitter could handle it. She walked into the adjoining bedroom and sat down on the bed, lying back and exhaling loudly, enjoying the solitude and summoning the energy to get her through the night. She lay there for just a few moments, her eyes closed, her skin still warm and damp in parts. She felt a bit of water run down her neck and it reminded her of a bug walking on her skin. She stood up quickly, removing the towel she had wrapped around her hair.

Picking up the plastic bag on the dresser, she removed the package of sheer black pantyhose. Cindy had decided in the store that she wouldn't wear panties with them. Tonight she wanted to feel sensual, her dress sliding smoothly over her hips and bottom.

She toweled her legs vigorously before easing the stockings on, pulling the rolled film up gently, careful not to run them. She ran her hand over the front of her stomach, almost hard and fairly flat from the sit-ups she had been doing faithfully each morning for the last few months. Her legs were still lean and taut from years of ballet. Slipping her feet into black stilettos, she almost tripped, laughing as she reached out to the wall to steady herself.

She paced around the bedroom, stopping to admire herself in the full-length mirror, turning her body sideways and admiring the line of her torso from shoulder to foot. The heels made her slimmer, her thighs and backside angled upward. Her breasts were not as high as they were before nursing Matt and MJ, Michael Junior, but they were firm and plump. She considered not wearing a bra with the dress and tried to recall how low the scoop on the neckline was.

She had a thought and opened the top drawer of the bureau quickly, running her hands over the tangled garments until she found it, the black silk chemise Mike had given her years ago on their first wedding anniversary. It was barely wrinkled, barely worn. How long had it been since she wore it? Since before MJ was born, before he was even on the way. In fact, she thought, smiling, the chemise was probably responsible for getting MJ started in the first place. She raised her arms over her head, anticipating the feel of silk slipping into place over her hips, but it stopped at her waist and she had to pull it down the rest of the way. Still, it fit. She would wear it and skip the bra.

She looked at herself again in the mirror and liked the unbroken look of black beginning with the chemise and ending with the high heels. Her hair was chin length now, bobbed evenly, and Cindy thought it made her look younger. She brushed her hair with quick, energetic strokes. Leaning over, she let her locks fall forward, and raised her hair dryer over it, the heat teasing the scalp of her head Finally, she flipped her head back to admire the fullness of the blonde mass as it settled around her face. She picked up the bottle of Chanel No. 5 perfume and had to pry the stopper a bit to remove it. Lifting the decanter to her nose, she was relieved that the scent was still fresh, not spoiled with age.

There was nothing left to do but put on her dress, but Cindy delayed.

She was hoping Mike might walk in and see her clad only in lingerie and stockings. It would be a moment that could put the evening on course. Picking up her watch, she checked the time, almost 7:15, before she fastened it around her wrist. Her anger with her husband swelled but she pushed it down even as she felt her jaw harden into argument position. She heard the car in the driveway, the slam of the side door, and the voices of the children as they ran to him. She knew Mike was picking up the boys, asking them if they'd been good today. Finally, she heard his voice at the bottom of the stairs, calling out jovially, "Sit down now, guys. I've got to get upstairs or Mom will kill me."

She listened to his footsteps coming up the stairs, two at a time, he was hurrying, and she readied herself to see him. He walked into the bedroom, his tie already undone and his fingers rapidly unbuttoning the blue shirt she had ironed that morning. "Sorry, sorry," he said perfunctorily. "The faculty meeting ran way over and I got stuck talking to Dean Levine afterwards about the Trustees visiting classes next week. She wants a couple of them to sit in on my social history class."

"That must mean she's heard good things about the class."

"I guess. That would sure be nice." There was relief in his voice. Clearly he had expected her to be angry.

He threw his clothes off hastily and stood now in his shorts and socks. Cindy liked his not too tall body. It was nicely proportioned, still tight and lean from squash, racquet ball, other gym activities she couldn't keep up with.

"I'll be quick in the shower," he said.

She wondered why Mike hadn't looked at her while he spoke. She walked towards him and stood in front of him, leaning in slowly to embrace him for just an instant, her arms somewhat loose around his neck, her chest not quite touching his. She was a little embarrassed; this kind of affection did not come easily to them any more. "Okay," she said, straining for lightness, "we should probably leave in about fifteen minutes."

He looked at her, surprised, and she smiled up at him, watching him look at her outfit, wondering if he'd recognize the chemise. He almost smiled back at her but she could see that his expression was more curious than admiring, his mouth not quite able to break into an open grin. He said, joking, "Isn't it a little cold out for that?" running his forefinger against her bare shoulder before turning and walking into the bathroom.

Standing perfectly still, Cindy stared at her husband until he shut the bathroom door. Then she went to the closet and found her black cocktail dress. She put it on, leaving the zipper in the back open. She would wait and ask Mike to zip it. The dress was elegant because of its simplicity, a sheath with tiny sleeves cutting across the slope of her shoulders at a sultry angle. It hung to just below the knee, but she practiced sitting on the bed and crossing her legs so that part of her thighs showed.

She heard the water go on in the shower and waited a few seconds before she moved soundlessly to the heap of Mike's clothes next to the bed. The wallet was first, but it held only his driver's license, an old photo of the boys, money, a ticket stub from a Bulls game. Other pockets produced keys, a receipt for candy or gum, something that cost seventy-nine cents, and a scrap of paper that said, "Return library books" on it. Cindy was careful to return everything to its proper place. Looking in the mirror, she was startled by her nervous expression, the odd twist of her mouth. She pressed her palms against her cheeks and felt the heat of her shame. Sighing heavily, she sank onto the bed and fixed her eyes on the bathroom door.

Cindy had felt uneasy all that day, since early that morning while at the supermarket. Shopping with her sons was never easy. Matt was only three and sat in the front of the cart while MJ, two years older, sat in the back and waited for opportunities to pull Matt's hair while Cindy selected items off the shelves. Today, while reaching for a carton of milk, she heard a smashing of glass and realized with horror that the sound came from near her own grocery cart. Cranberry juice was running down the aisle and MJ was cowering in the back of the cart shouting, "It was Matt! It was Matt!" She had waited sheepishly while the stock boy mopped up the tart-smelling red liquid and swept up the glass. Apologizing continually, she turned a steadfast glare on MJ.

It was lousy luck that Debbie Marshall strolled by. Cindy did her best to appear unflapped, calling out to her neighbor, "Never a dull moment!" Debbie didn't stop to talk, but made a wide berth with her cart to avoid the mess, all the while giving Cindy a smile laden with too much sympathy for the immediate situation. Cindy was reminded of a similar look from Ed Runell, a colleague of Mike's in the history department, when she had run into him at the gas station a couple of weeks ago. He had asked her how she was with such concern in his voice, his milky blue eyes searching her face, that Cindy had stopped for a moment to think if anyone in her extended family had died recently.

For days after, she had watched Mike for a sign, something that would alarm or assure her. She rummaged through the papers in his study and checked the pockets of his clothes, but there was nothing. I'd know, *I'd know* if something were, if he were, but he's not, so forget it. She had almost pushed the incident from her mind, but here was that look, that secretive, embarrassed look, from Debbie. And it seemed that Debbie, unlike Ed, didn't have the courage even to talk to Cindy, stepping around her widely as if Cindy had a disease that she didn't want to catch. Debbie made her way down the aisle, stopping to examine a box of crackers. Cindy watched her covertly, pretending to rearrange the items in her cart, mentally asking Debbie, *what do you think you know?* After Debbie's cart turned the corner, Cindy turned her own cart around, heading off in the other direction. She walked several steps before she realized she was trembling.

As she pushed the cart in front of the bakery at the back of the store, Cindy asked herself, incredulous, *is this how it happens?* Everyone pities the poor woman who's too dumb to notice that her husband's cheating? It was this idea of pity, almost more than the possibility of an affair, that upset Cindy. The thought of people talking about her and Mike, and Mike and . . . who? *Oh, my God*, she thought, *who?* She went through the possibilities, the couples whose children were friends with MJ and Matt. She remembered that once, at a barbecue last summer, Mike had hugged Bridget O'Donnell on the pretext that he loved her blueberry pie. But Bridget and her husband seemed close, very close. There were all the women who worked at the college; she only knew a handful. And then, no, he wouldn't be that stupid, would he? The lights in the store seemed to flicker with the pulse of her heart. Would Mike be dumb enough to get involved with a student? She shook her head. She wouldn't contemplate that. No. It was too sordid.

By the time Cindy got to the meat section, she felt so flushed she wanted to pick up a package of refrigerated ground round and hold it against her face. Her sons were fighting again in the grocery cart but she didn't admonish them. She stroked the sandy blonde cowlick standing off the back of Matt's head as he wiggled, restless in the cart. It was painful to even look at MJ, the image of Mike, who had taken advantage of Cindy's distraction to open a package of Oreo cookies, chocolate drool covering his chin. Cindy watched him and felt the corners of her eyes become hot with tears. She fought them, searching through the jumble in her purse for a tissue. Good God, she thought, what if Debbie strolled by now and caught me crying all over the groceries? She blinked her eyes to quell the tears and lowered her head.

She wheeled the grocery cart into the check-out lane and was confronted with the gossip tabloids. Headlines about Madonna's flirting with the Pope leapt at her from the magazine racks. She started to laugh, the heaviness in her chest expelled like a geyser into the air, freeing her. Now the idea of Mike having an affair seemed as ludicrous as Madonna chasing the Pope. She was overreacting. People like her and Mike didn't behave like that, they just didn't. What was she getting all worked up about?

Even as she told herself this, a tiny corner of her mind remained cautious. She assured herself that if something were going on, she could simply correct the situation, if there was anything to correct. Probably not. Oh, people might have noticed the glimmer of a flirtation between Mike and someone, people will say *anything*, but what man or woman was innocent of that? Hadn't Cindy had to endure winks and overly-pressured hugs from Rick Snyder, a colleague of Mike's, for years? Perhaps people had gossiped about her and Rick. She laughed to herself, the idea of her and Rick so absurd.

When she got to the parking lot, however, she noticed Debbie two aisles over loading groceries into her car. Cindy remembered the look on Debbie's face, that wary, awkward expression when they'd met in the store, and felt her blood quicken. Now, minutes before leaving for the dinner party, her pulse was still racing. Mike was so blasé at the sight of her in the chemise, so uncomfortable in her embrace. The phone rang, jolting her, and Cindy looked at it with annoyance. She picked the receiver up on the third ring.

"Hello?" She realized her voice sounded frightened. Snap out of it! She told herself.

"Mrs. Dyson? Hi, this is Dean Mira Levine. Is Mike there?"

"Yes," she paused, suddenly confused about what to say. She remembered this Mira, a petite woman with frizzy hair who wore Birkenstocks. They'd met at some barbecue. "He's in the shower," Cindy finally answered. "Can I take a message?" She reached for her purse to find a pen.

"It's kind of involved. Just tell him to call me back at my office. Thanks."

"Dean Levine?"

"Call me Mira."

"Thank you. Mira. We're going out in a few minutes. Is it all right if Mike calls you back later tonight?"

There was a pause and the airy sound of her breathing. "I guess so. Well, do you know how late? I'm meeting a job candidate later. Just let him know I need to get in touch with him about the trustees' visit next week. I'm sorry to bother you at home, but . . ."

"Oh, that's all right. Mike is so excited about the trustees sitting in on his class."

"Pardon me?"

"His class. Mike told me that you spoke to him about the trustees observing him in the classroom. He's flattered."

The line was silent a moment and Cindy felt her cheeks flush. Mira laughed awkwardly and said, "I'm so busy; I don't know what I've said to whom. Just tell him to call me when he can."

"I'll tell him."

Cindy hung up the phone. For several moments, she drummed the heel of her shoe into the floor. At some point, she realized her foot felt sore. She wiped her damp palms on the sides of her dress and let out a rush of air.

She opened the bathroom door. Mike had been in there too long. The air clouded in steamy columns and the mirror was sweating with moisture.

Cindy shouted, "Hurry up! We're supposed to be there in five minutes."

"Coming, coming," Mike called back, sounding besieged, and Cindy heard the water shut off. "Who was that on the phone?" he asked.

"Mira Levine. About the trustees. She seemed surprised to hear they were sitting in on your class." She listened to his silence, to its weight, but then he said, "Hey, Cin? There's no towels in here."

She went into the hallway, grabbed a towel from the linen closet and returned to the bathroom. Pushing open the sliding door on the bath tub, Mike reached for the towel and began to mop the moisture from his naked skin. "Thanks," he said, now putting a foot on the side of the bath tub to towel between his toes. When Cindy didn't respond, he looked up and said, "Say, you look great."

"Yeah? You look like a cheating husband."

Lifting the towel and wrapping it around his waist, he looked at the floor but then lifted his eyes to hers. "I'm not going to lie to you, Cin. Yeah. I met someone."

"You *met* someone?" She tried to laugh but her throat closed. "I meet people all the time. Doesn't mean I sleep with them. Get dressed. Hurry up."

His head pulled back in surprise. "You still want to go? Look, why don't we talk—"

"Get dressed. Move it." She walked back into the bedroom.

Reaching one arm over her shoulder and the other around her waist, she zipped the dress with a swift, even motion. Sitting at her vanity, she emptied her cosmetic bag. Selecting a pert red lipstick, she coated her lips twice. With the same lipstick, she placed a few dots on her cheeks and rubbed the color until it highlighted her skin with a garnet blush. She rummaged through the compacts and small vials in front of her and picked up a black eye liner pencil, rimming her eyelids to accentuate the almond-shape of her blue eyes. A tear had spilled down each cheek and she flicked both off with a swipe of her index fingers. Opening her jewelry box, she reached for the pearl earrings she had decided earlier to wear. She changed her mind and selected the large turquoise dangles that swung easily on her ears. "Mexico," she would say when someone complimented her, "Mike bought these for me on our honeymoon." She brushed her hair one last time and shaped it to her liking with her hands. Finally, she stood, light-headed at the sight of herself in the glass. No one, she thought, not a single person, will feel sorry for me.

LOCKERS

Even before she set foot in her classroom where she'd taught eighth grade English for almost three decades, Lena heard their voices. Ryan Simmons, the new principal, speaking slowly, stretching his words out in his characteristic way to give himself time to think. Albert Johnson, the vice principal for at least a decade, with a higher, quick voice, his sentences turning up at the end to sound like questions. It was that lack of committing to anything, Lena knew, that had kept him from getting the job of principal each time the position had been available.

What were they doing in her room so early in the school day? She stood in the corridor and positioned herself to the side of the open door, her shoulders pressed against the wall. She could tell that the men were at the back of the classroom, though it was easy to hear them because they both spoke loudly, as if they were giving speeches in a stadium.

"Whoa, what a mess!" Ryan said. "Is every locker filled with garbage?"

The sound of metal doors being opened. Albert said, "At least a few of them? Five or six?"

"Man. She should go on that hoarding TV show."

"Oh, yeah? My wife watches that show?"

"Looks like a bunch of travel stuff. That's strange."

Inhaling, Lena strode into the classroom. "Good morning," she said briskly. "Can I help you with something?" She continued over to her desk, putting the sling of her messenger bag over the side of her chair and removing her coat.

He knocked on one of the locker doors and said, "Inventory."

She raised her eyebrows. "You're taking inventory of these lockers?"

Walking to her desk, Ryan said, "Not the contents, the lockers themselves. We're selling them to a health spa. Most of them, anyway. Some are in too rough a shape."

Albert seemed uncertain whether he should remain at the lockers or join Ryan. He walked half-way to the front of the room and stood beside a student desk, placing his hand on it flatly as if to keep it from rising from the floor.

"Selling? Why?"

"We don't need them," Ryan said, more speed in his words than usual. "There've been lockers in the corridors for, what?" He looked at Albert, "Fifteen years?"

"Yup. Fifteen years," Albert nodded continually as he spoke. "It was the same year we got the new tables in the cafeteria? A big levy passed that year?"

Glancing at the back of the room, Lena frowned and said, "A health spa wants these filthy, old lockers?"

"Yup. They may be filthy and old, but they're a lot wider than the ones on the market now. Fresh coat of paint in some trendy color and they'll be good as new."

Ryan slipped his hand into his pockets and scanned the top of her desk, piled with tidy stacks of paper. He reached for her paperweight, a Murano glass millefiori, and tossed it from one hand to the other and back again.

Holding out her palm, Lena said, "Careful, please." He disregarded her hand and set it back on her desk.

"No one uses the lockers, Lena. Except you. You're going to have to clear that stuff out."

Some of the teachers referred to Ryan as "Young Whippersnapper." He'd taught for only three years before beginning the climb up the administrative ladder. He wasn't the staff's first choice but he was the candidate willing to relocate to Cleveland.

"Ryan, I've been teaching for almost thirty-five years, most of them here in Cleveland Heights. I have a *lot* of curricular materials. And I teach English, a humanities discipline. Materials don't become dated or irrelevant like they do in some other subjects." She realized how teacherly she sounded, as if she were explaining things to her eighth graders.

"I appreciate that, Lena" he said, "but you've got a situation back there." He waved back and forth with a pointed finger.

"A situation? It's hardly a *situation*."

He lifted his hands as if to surrender. "Fine. You've just got a mess of travel books and magazines back there."

Lena felt heat on her neck and was glad she was wearing a turtleneck. "I use examples of travel writing from time to time when teaching descriptive essay writing." She hoped she sounded convincing.

Ryan pressed his lips and breathed air through his nostrils in hyphenated sniffs. "Look, someone from the spa is coming on Friday to take a look at the lockers. Make sure yours are empty by then."

"Friday?" She'd blurted out the word. She clasped her hands and said more softly, "That's not a lot of time. There's a lot to sort through and grades are almost due."

"Just pick what you really need and toss the rest of the stuff out. You can't need that many examples of travel writing. I can get one of the custodians to help you."

"No!" She hurled the word from her mouth like a ball of ice. Ryan looked as if he'd been struck. Quickly, she said, "No, thank you. It's not junk and it can't just be tossed. You may not be able to make heads or tails of it, but I know exactly what's in there."

Ryan pressed his fingertips together and said, "Fine, but have everything out by Friday. Find another place for it."

"Well, Ryan, do you have any room in your office?"

His eyes enlarged behind his wire-frame glasses, just for a second. Waving his index finger at her, he shook his head in mock acquiescence. "That's what I like about you, Lena. Your sense of humor."

"Your sense of humor?" Albert followed Ryan out of the classroom.

Lena waited until she could no longer hear their voices. She hung up her coat in the narrow closet behind her desk and sat down. Holding her head in her hands, she heard the first bell ring which meant students could enter the building and go into the cafeteria for breakfast or to the library to read. She stood and approached the lockers. They seemed to stand at attention, a dozen elongated metal soldiers. They were wide, that was true. When she first came to teach here, students shared the lockers. Lena had appreciated their roominess when she began to fill them with travel guides and magazines. *Fodor's, Let's Go, The Lonely Planet, Italy on a Budget.* Within a year, she'd filled two lockers. Then she started going to used bookstores to search for old *Baedekers.* She loved the compact heft of the volumes, the stylized print on their covers. Yes, some of the pages were musty and mildewed but Lena brought the books to her nose and smelled the past, the knowable, non-threatening past. Most of the glossy *Condé Nast* magazines were from garage sales and flea markets. She'd collected almost twenty years of the journal, her favorite. During free moments in her classroom, she looked at the glossy covers depicting pyramids and beaches and mountains and her eyes welled up. She turned the pages, excited to see the article, photograph, or even the ad on the next slick and shiny page. In an issue from 1988, there was a photo of an attractive young couple holding hands and laughing as they ran through the Piazza San Marco, pigeons taking flight around them. She'd looked at this photo so often, she attributed some of the fraying of the page to her gazes. There were other images in the journals that she treasured, but this was her favorite. The man reminded her of her husband, Will, as a young man, with those long, strong limbs moving with such ease, ready to run a marathon.

"Morning!"

Startled, Lena turned to see Jen, her friend who taught eighth grade math in the classroom across the hall.

"Morning. How are you?" Lena said, closing the locker and hearing the syncopated click as the door latched.

"Not bad. Are you okay?" Jen studied Lena's face. "Your face is red. Hot flash?"

Laughing, Lena said, "No. Just angry. I walked into my room today to find Ryan and Albert going through my lockers. Did you know they're going to remove all the classroom lockers and sell them to a spa?"

"Are they? Well, I don't use mine. They're a waste of space in my classroom. I think the teachers should get a cut of the sale, though." Jen winked.

"That'll be the day. Good weekend?"

"Not bad. Yours?"

Lena walked to her desk and sat down. "Will took another fall on Saturday morning. We were in the emergency room for hours."

"No! Is he okay?"

"Yeah, but he's got a bad bruise on his cheek," Lena touched her own, "and we thought he might've broken his wrist. Luckily, it's just a bad sprain."

"Ouch. Poor Will."

"Well, you know Will. He never complains. He's determined to get out and do some walking today. At least once around the block."

"Did he fall because of the Parkinson's?"

"I don't know. Hard to say. I cleared all the area rugs from the first floor, just in case. I think he might've slid on one and couldn't regain his balance."

"Oh?"

Lena shrugged. "Will says no. Says he was just walking too fast, but who knows? He made me promise not to tell Travis."

"Did you call Travis?"

"No, but he called us on Sunday."

"How is he?"

Nodding, Lena said, "Great. Very excited about becoming a father. Oh, there's news! They know it's a girl."

"A girl? You're going to have a granddaughter? Congratulations!"

Clasping her hands, Lena said, "Thanks, I can't wait. Just wish Travis and Blythe lived closer to us. We'll be flying out to the West Coast every chance we get after the baby is born."

"Well, speaking of flying, I'd better. Have a good morning. I'll bop in at lunch."

"It's Monday. How good can it be?"

The biggest factor in how the day went, of course, was the students. In her twenties, Lena had shed some tears in the staff bathroom more times than she could count. A colleague's barb was hurtful but a student lashing out at her was more wounding. Over the years, she'd toughened, like everyone did, but that wasn't always a good thing. She realized how easy it was to shut a mouthy student down. The girl whose response to every reminder to do her work, "Oh, my God!" was shocked when Lena once repeated the words back to her in a falsetto, following with, "I'm very flattered but there's no need to call me 'my God.' You can call me Mrs. Meyer." The other students laughed and the girl blushed up to her hairline. She didn't know that Lena's heart sank, that she chastised herself for taking a shortcut, one that hurt the student. The girl didn't know that she heard, "Oh, my God!" at least twenty times a day, every day. At nine in the morning, you ignored it. By mid-day, you sighed and raised your eyebrows. By two-thirty, you wanted to tell a student to just knock it off. If you could quiet one student, just one, make her an example to scare a few others into being quiet so she could teach, damn it, actually *teach*, wasn't it okay? No, it wasn't. She'd admonished herself for weeks and went out of her way to be ridiculously kind to the girl, as if she could will her to sing out, "Oh, my God!" again. She never did. A boy would've relented, but girls? Girls could hold a grudge.

Lena picked up a stack of papers and began placing one on every desk. With a marker, she wrote on the whiteboard, *Read the excerpt from the article, "Components of an Informational Speech" and answer the questions on the back of the paper in complete sentences. When you finish, start reading the chapter in your text on "Information Versus Persuasion."*

"Hi, Mrs. Meyer."

"Good morning, Jayden. How are you?"

"Hel-lo! What are we doing today?"

"Hello, Richard. Take your seat and read the instructions on the board."

She stepped into the doorway and looked at a group of students clustered in the hall in front of the lockers. "C'mon, people. The bell is about to ring."

Several students streamed past her. She heard Josh Clemens bellow, "What do we got to do?"

"Hi, Mrs. Meyer!"

"Hello, Alexandra. Come take your seat."

At ten minutes after eight, she shut the door and walked to the front of the classroom. "I hope you all had a good weekend. If you haven't already started reading the article excerpt on your desks, begin now. If you have, good for you. The questions on the back shouldn't take very long, but be sure you answer in *complete* sentences."

"What do we got to do?"

"As I just said Josh, read the article on your desk and answer the questions on the back. The instructions are also here, on the board." She pointed.

He lifted the paper. "This? This is the article?"

"Yes, that's it."

"And then what?"

"Turn the paper over and answer the questions on the back."

"We got to do this for homework if we don't finish?"

"You'll finish. It's just an excerpt. This should take no more than ten minutes. We have a lot to do today, so get started."

Waving the paper like a flag, he said, "We got to do the questions alone or are we going to do them as a class?"

"Answer them on your own and then we'll discuss them as a class."

"Can we change the answers if we got them wrong?"

"You're not there yet, Josh. Just *read* the article for now."

He looked at her and then at his desk. She continued, "If you finish before the others, start reading the next chapter in your text on—"

Josh looked up. "We got to do that, too?"

Lena sighed and then spoke slowly, raising her voice a bit to address

the entire class, "*If* you finish and others are still working, start reading the chapter, "Information Versus Persuasion," in your textbook."

Richard snorted. "Don't worry, Josh. You'll never finish early."

Josh turned in his seat. "Shut up, dude."

"Josh," Lena said, "you've got work to do."

She saw the look of injustice flash across his face, his triangular nostrils becoming more pointed. He called out, "Rich is telling me I'm not going to finish—"

"You won't if you keep talking."

An immediate, collective, "*Ouuuuuuuhhhhh*" carpeted the classroom.

Josh half-rose and looked at his classmates with disgust but Lena saw the soft tremor of his chin when he said, "Hey, you all shut up."

"Just get to work, Josh."

"This is *school*. We're *supposed* to ask questions in school."

"Yes, I've answered your questions, Josh. Get down to work now."

"Why aren't you yelling at him for what he said to me?"

"Josh, I don't even remember what he said, but you—"

"He said I'm never gonna finish early."

"Mrs. Meyer?" Tammy said. "Would you tell Josh to be quiet. Because I can't concentrate."

"Me either," a couple students said together, happy to voice a legitimate complaint although Lena knew they didn't care about Josh's talking.

"Okay, let's all be quiet and concentrate. Josh, if you have a question, see me *at my desk*." She spoke the last words slowly and heavily, laying a verbal wall around her desk. She was hoping to finish grading the grammar tests so she could pass them out to be taken home and signed by parents. She normally never graded during class but the hours in the emergency room on Saturday cost her time. She'd spent most of Sunday watching Will while pretending not to, wondering if he really was as unworried and relaxed as he seemed to be, listening to Puccini arias, *The New York Times* spread about him as he sat on the couch, his feet on the coffee table. She noticed that he held his coffee cup in his left hand, the one without the tremor.

Lowering his head, Josh said, "*Daaamn*. This is too long."

Swayla blurted, "Mrs. Meyers, Josh said 'damn.'"

Mrs. Meyers put a finger to her lips.

"I'm just saying," she spoke with exasperation, "that he said—"

"We all heard him, Swayla. You don't have to repeat it."

"So you don't care that someone's swearing in class?"

Lena scanned the classroom. "Has anyone finished reading the article and answering the questions?"

Two hands went up. Jack and Aleesha. So dependable. Nodding, Lena looked at them and said, "Good. Excellent use of time. Everyone else, finish up." She noted the surprised expressions on some faces that a couple of their classmates were already done with the assignment. Lena had learned that early. Switch gears. Underscore how inappropriate the behavior was by praising the kids who reliably did what they were supposed to. It worked, even on eighth graders. They were still just kids, competitive, vulnerable kids.

She sat at her desk and opened her drawer, removing her colored pens. She noted errors in noun and verb agreement in green, possessive and plural errors in purple, spelling errors in blue, passive voice errors in orange. There was a theory that consistent color coding increased comprehension and Lena was game to try anything that could do that. The only time she used red ink was for punctuation errors, errors there was no excuse for making in eighth grade. Jack and Aleesha had perfect papers. She picked up a yellow highlighter and drew big smiley faces on the top of the papers. She rounded them with sunny rays and wrote, "Awesome!" next to "100%." She felt like writing, "Thank you!" Was she helping them to become good writers or was it their innate intelligence that made them do well in her class, in every class? Over the years, she'd saved notes from former students who'd written to thank her, who'd professed that she'd been their favorite teacher. Maybe one day she'd receive notes from Jack and Aleesha. Would she still be teaching? More likely retired, caring for Will and missing her classroom and these very students, the majority of whom would rather be somewhere, anywhere, else.

Lena glanced at Josh before saying, "Okay. You should all be finished now. You've had plenty of time. Let's discuss the main points of this article."

An echoing crash followed by, "Owww!"

Tony Hallinger had leaned back in his seat, knocking his head into one of the lockers.

Amidst some giggles, Lena asked, "Are you okay, Tony?"

Rubbing his head, the boy said, "*Damn*, that hurt!"

Swayla opened her mouth and Lena said immediately, "Read the first question for us, Swayla."

Second period was a planning period, a gift. It made the first period of the day bearable. Fifty minutes of thirteen and fourteen-year-olds and then a respite. She had so much grading to do. She wanted to turn in her quarter grades early, on Friday, so the upcoming weekend was free. She and Will were scheduled to attend what his doctor called "Parkinson's camp." It was a chance for family and caretakers to learn more about the condition, to ask questions, and to meet others in the area who also had the disease in its advanced stages. Will had resisted going, but Lena was hoping to meet other spouses of patients. It was time to face the word: caretaker. She had fears she couldn't quite articulate to herself, let alone to Will. But she knew it was time to at least listen, to hear the stories of other caretakers.

Five years ago, when her husband was first diagnosed, she'd read everything she could find about Parkinson's. She'd stay awake in bed wishing she could turn back the clock, have her husband's condition diagnosed at an earlier stage, a time when they might have been able to take steps to slow its progression. And they should have done things they wouldn't be able to do even in the near future. Travel! All the talk about Venice over the years, where they'd gone on their honeymoon and fantasized about returning to after they both retired. Lena remembered those two weeks following their marriage, walking on the Rialto in the late afternoon, sunshine on one side of the bridge, shadows on the other. She'd admired a scarf that seemed to swirl with the water and sky of the city, and Will insisted on buying it for her. They entered every shop on the Piazza San Marco, Will buying her earrings, a cameo necklace, the paperweight on her desk. In the pensione, he'd introduced her to the staff as, "My bride," his arm cradling her shoulders. And then they'd gone to Burano and fallen in love with the vividly painted houses, the fresh laundry drying on lines strung from the windows. They agreed to learn Italian, to come back again and again, to not be taken for tourists, all the things people say when they're a bit mad with joy. Flying home, Will had whispered a favorite line of Browning's to Lena on the plane, "Open my heart and you will see . . . engraved inside . . . Italy!" And then he kissed her, the stewardess waiting to set coffee on their trays.

Now, when she managed to sleep, Lena had a recurrent dream about walking with Will on a winding, narrow stone walk, her husband losing his balance and falling into a canal. She woke in a panic, certain she'd stopped breathing in her sleep. The slight shake of the mattress was enough to semi-rouse Will. He'd roll toward her, his hand cupping her shoulder, sometimes slipping down to find her breast, the constant tremor in his fingers and his wrist somehow soothing, rocking her back to sleep.

She often reminded herself that Will was still Will. There were some difficulties but ones handled with simple accommodations. They'd traded in their stick-shift car for an automatic. They'd put a guard rail on the side of the shower. They made sure he wore only non-skid shoes, soles with traction.

But this last year was different even if Will wouldn't admit it. A slip in the shower, despite the guard rail, spilled groceries in a parking lot, the realization that he should no longer ride his bike, no matter how slowly. A few nights ago, Lena had sat at her laptop and instead of Googling the terms, "*Parkinson's rate progression*" had typed in the search bar, "*Please cure my husband's disease.*" A prayer to the internet. She hadn't been to church since she was a teen.

She tidied the pile of the first period's speech assignments and opened her grade book. Calculating the letter grade was a cinch. Much more time would be spent writing the accompanying comments on each report card, in part because Lena allowed herself to fantasize about what she really wanted to write. *Tallis seems to have a permanent scowl on her face. Does she suffer from digestive issues? Jeremiah's pants need a good hoist up his backside; a belt may do the trick.*

"Knock, knock," Sharon's voice rang out. The principal's secretary entered, pulling a paper from a manila folder. "Ryan wants this by the end of the day."

"Are you serious? What is it?"

Sharon put the paper on Lena's desk. "A survey. He wants some input before the school board meeting tomorrow night."

"Input on what?" Lena said, realizing how much she sounded like Josh. She groaned. "Never mind. I'll just read it."

Sharon smiled tightly and said, "Don't kill the messenger," as she left the classroom.

"Sorry," Lena called after her. She looked at the paper and read the first lines: "As we proceed with our anti-bullying campaign, I'd like a deeper sense of our student body. Teacher input, as always, is invaluable. Please share your observations as to student archetypes and the roles they play in individual and group instances of bullying. DO NOT MENTION SPECIFIC NAMES. Rather, approximate the number of students in each of your classes you deem ringleaders, accomplices, and targets. When possible, use specific scenarios and language to apprise me of troublesome situations. Again, DO NOT MENTION SPECIFIC NAMES. I also ask that you DO NOT DISCUSS what you've written with colleagues. From time to time, parents complain about the suspected lack of discretion amongst our staff."

Rolling her head back, Lena mouthed the words, *kill me.*

The fact was the most seasoned teachers immediately recognized types of students. Within moments of entering a classroom, Lena generally knew who was smart, who was a troublemaker, who was unduly quiet, and who was scary. Sure, every now and then a student surprised her, took a turn and landed in a new category, but it was rare.

The smart ones were the best ones, obviously, the ones who participated and cooperated in class, who made connections between literature and life, who had a sense of the future. In a few years, they'd want to get into the Ivy League or the most competitive colleges but their identities were already wrapped up with being among the smartest. The negative aspect of this group was that it also included the goody-two-shoes, those students who annoyed her with their offers to help when their motivation was usually self-serving. They weren't so much the problem as their parents, especially the mothers who called to argue why a grade was an A and not an A+. Last year, when Zach Tryton's unemployed and highly educated mother called six times in a month to explain that her son wasn't socially awkward, he just preferred to give "full responses, answers indicative of an advanced mind," Lena had replied, her voice veiled with professional concern, "I appreciate thoroughness even though I sometimes have to urge Zach to achieve closure. On another matter, could you see to it that he carries tissues or a handkerchief? I'm worried that his putting his fingers in his nose and then his mouth so frequently is off-putting to the other students and that may be hampering him socially." That brief moment of silence on the other end of the phone had been unduly satisfying. Then the woman spoke in a rush about poor Zach suffering from allergies, as if he didn't have enough to deal with, being so unusually gifted.

The troublemakers. In earlier years, Lena referred to them as the "challenging," but she was as burned out by these students as any other teacher on staff. When they were younger instructors, they'd been determined to make inroads with this crowd, all too ready to believe that a home situation was the reason for Tallis's haughty disdain or Josh's constant interruptions, or Richard's failed attempts at being the class clown. But these last few years, Lena didn't care why they were acting out. Tallis wasn't just Tallis. She was the girl who had been glaring at Lena for thirty years. Richard was only the last in a long line of guys who thought he had a future career in stand-up comedy. He'd looked puzzled that time she'd finally told him, "You need new material." Students like Josh weren't really that bad, just annoying with their constant interruptions. Yes, anxious about falling behind, but unable to figure out quieter coping strategies. Sighing, she knew that was her job. She had to cut Josh some slack, give him more help in a manner that didn't invite Richard's attention.

The quiet ones, they were the ones that worried Lena. They didn't clamor for attention; they ran from it. They slouched in their seats and avoided her gaze. Lena felt intuitively that they were harboring disturbing or sad secrets. They were like cats. If she approached them too quickly, they ran scared. If she was patient, writing encouraging comments on their papers, giving them a quick smile in class, a couple might come to her and ask for help. When she earned their trust, she might hear a detail about their private lives. An alcoholic mother, a father who went out to fill the car's gas tank four days ago and wasn't back yet. One of her students suspected that the sixth grader who looked just like him was his half-sibling. Other teachers sent these students to the guidance counselor but Lena didn't. If one of these quiet students mustered the courage to speak to Lena, she wasn't going to pawn the student off on someone else. As painful as school was for these students, their homes were worse. She encouraged the quiet ones to spend time at the public library, a place where they could sit at a table and not stand out. They were old enough to be there alone and could spend hours with no one bothering them. Lena got to know the librarians, told them who she was sending, and to not question them unless they asked for research help. She knew that simple solitude was a gift for them.

Over the years, there'd been several students who'd frightened her. The brilliant but lazy loner with the stray hairs on his upper lip who did his work quickly and then drew violent cartoons in his notebook. It was all too easy to imagine him pulling a gun from his backpack. The hulking, know-it-all boy who sat on the edge of his seat, ready to pounce if Lena made a mistake, if she mispronounced a student's name or forgot to change the date on the class calendar. He didn't understand why he was friendless and she sensed his frustration. She imagined he felt trapped, that he knew high school wasn't going to be any different, that he'd never have his classmates' approval no matter how many times he proved a teacher wrong. Lena wanted to tell him that he was in a prison of his own making but she stalled at the thought of entering that prison. She gave his name to the guidance counselor, his and others who sat in class with expressions on their faces that were too blank or too fraught.

Sometimes she wondered if any of them knew the truth about themselves. Did the troublemakers know they were troublemakers? There were days she longed to tell them, "Maybe you weren't in the past and you won't be in the future, but now, right now, you are in the troublemakers' category. Try to get out of it. For your sake and mine."

Lena fingered the corner of the survey. Ryan hadn't served his time in the trenches, abandoning teaching for administration the first chance he got. Sure, he threw around words like "archetypes," but he didn't deserve the knowledge gained from painstaking lessons that took their toll year after year. Picking up her red pen, Lena wrote: *I think it's ill-advised to categorize students. During the course of my teaching career, I've observed that one student can play many roles. Victims become victimizers. Accomplices are promoted to key bullying positions. Rather than share anecdotal evidence of specific instances of various behaviors, I suggest we focus on a broad educational campaign to eliminate all aspects of inappropriate behavior.* She signed her name in large letters and then noted in parentheses, *I assume it's permissible to mention my own name?* She knew she'd gone too far, but she'd written in pen. Good, she thought. No backing down.

She opened her bottom drawer and fished her phone out of her purse, dialing her home number. She had to share this with Will. He'd laugh and say, "Bravo!" quelling the nerves already stacking up in her chest. Listening to the phone ring, the nerves rose into her throat, an image of Will lying on the sidewalk, no one around to help, taking shape in her mind. *Answer, honey, answer.*

"Can you believe it?" Jen entered the room waving her copy of the questionnaire.

Lena heard her husband's voice inviting the caller to leave a message and turned the phone off. "Oh, I'm already done. Here, read what I wrote."

Scanning the paper, Jen's eyes widened. Her mouth became a shocked tunnel, open and dark, and she covered it with one hand. She heaved with laughter, silent at first, and then spilling from her. "You are going to be in *so much trou-ble*, Mrs. Meyer!"

Lena cupped her chin, enjoying how incredulous Jen looked. "This is such baloney. Ryan wants to wax poetic to the school board about all his new initiatives. Bullying's been a part of school life since forever. You see it, you do something about it, pronto. You don't write about archetypes."

Jen leaned against the edge of the desk, running her tongue over her lips. "Yeah, Ryan's the bully with that early retirement bull. Promise me you won't retire before I do."

"I'm not going anywhere." Lena put her phone back in her purse and closed the drawer.

"Okay. We agree. We leave together when we want to and not a moment before."

Nodding, Lena said "Well, Will had to leave work years before we planned on it, so we need my salary."

"Oh, right. Sorry. None of my business, but I hope he got a good severance package from the air traffic control plant?"

"Could've been better."

"Well, Joe will never retire."

"You don't think so?"

"He'd go crazy at home. He drives *me* crazy on the weekends."

Lena smiled. She'd been hearing Jen's tales of her husband, a successful plumber who could only sit still for a football game, for years.

"Aw, you and Joe are happy together."

Jen yawned, raising her arms over her head. "After all these years, I'm not sure what that even means."

Will on the sidewalk, the image sprouted immediately in Lena's mind. When you're about to lose happiness, you know what it means, Lena thought.

❦   ❦   ❦

Third period. The students were fully awake by this time of the day, livelier than first period. Several came through the door after the bell rang. Immediately, Justin Williams said, "Can I go to my locker? I don't got a pencil."

"I don't *have* a pencil," Lena said.

"Me either."

"Can I go, too? I forgot my book."

"Mrs. Meyer, I didn't get a chance to get a drink. Can I go get a drink?"

Lena walked to the white board and put her finger to her lips. "Okay, listen to what I have to say before anyone goes anywhere. You each have an article excerpt on your desk, titled, "Components of an Informational

Speech." Read it carefully and then answer the questions on the back of the page. Make sure you answer the questions in complete sentences. I've written the directions here on the board as well. If you finish before the rest of the class, open your text to the chapter on "Information Versus Persuasion" and start reading it. Are there any questions?"

"Can I get a pencil now?" Justin asked.

Lena lifted her hand, palm outward, to halt the other students who were starting to speak and asked, "Are there any questions about these assignments? No? Okay, get started. Yes, Justin, you may get a pencil. Yes, Eli, you may get your book. No, DJ, you can't get a drink."

"But I'm thirsty!"

"We all are, but I can't have twenty-five people in the hallway getting a drink."

"I'm only one person."

"If I let you go, everyone else will expect to go. That's the definition of 'inevitable'."

"Awww, man!"

"Get to work, DJ, and the period will be over before you know it."

Lena could tell from the overly alert expression on Jessica Freedman's face that she was searching for a way to procrastinate. Jessica, Queen of the Troublemakers. She'd actually been quiet these first few minutes of class, surprising.

"Mrs. Meyer, I like your sweater." The girl's voice was chirpy.

The first volley. Lena answered quietly "Thank you."

"I really do!"

"Yes, I heard you. Time to get to work."

Jessica's eyes moved left to right. "What are we supposed to do?"

Lena gestured to the board and Jessica put a familiar whine in her voice and said, "I can't see the board. Can I change my seat?" She straightened in her chair and pointed, "Can I sit where Owen is?"

"I'm not switching with you. Mrs. Meyer, I'm not switching with her."

Walking in quick strides to Jessica's desk, Lena said, "Read this article. When you're finished, turn your paper over and answer the questions on the back."

"That's a really pretty sweater, Ms. Meyer."

Lena nodded and turned.

Louder, she said, "*I said* . . . that's a really pretty sweater, Mrs. Meyer."

Owen turned in his seat, his eyes squinting, and said, "You already said that."

Jessica, so attractive with those large indigo eyes and so aware of it, spat out, "I really like her sweater, okay? Is it a *crime* to like a sweater?"

"Okay, Jessica. Enough about my sweater. Read the article quietly or I'll send you to read it in the office."

Jessica didn't realize it was an empty threat. Since Ryan arrived, Lena had stopped sending students to the office. He fancied himself a conflict mediator but most of the teachers complained about the voluminous paperwork that resulted from any office referral.

The door opened and Justin entered the room. "I don't got no pencils in my locker."

Lena walked to her desk and opened her top drawer. She found a pencil and handed it to Justin, saying, "I don't have any pencils in my locker."

"That's what I said."

"Return this to me when class is over."

"I can't keep it?"

"No. Sorry. Other students will be asking for pencils in later classes."

He took the pencil and walked to his desk, staring down at the essay as he sat. "Say, Mrs. Meyer, what do we got to do?"

❧   ❧   ❧

Answer, answer, answer your phone. Lena looked at the clock. Eleven-thirty. The recording beeped and she said, "Hi, Sweetie, where are you? I tried earlier, too. Are you out walking? Please text me so I know you're okay. My lunch ends at noon." Slipping the phone into the pocket of her skirt, she picked up the questionnaire and headed out of the classroom.

In the office, she said, "Here you go," as she handed the questionnaire to Sharon.

"Done already? Wow. You're fast. I'll give it to Ryan."

"Thanks. Can I have a box of pencils?"

"Oh, we're all out. I put an order in but we won't have them until next Monday."

"We should all buy stock in pencils."

"Tell me about it."

"There she is! Hold up, Lena," Ryan called as he stepped from his adjoining office into Sharon's workspace.

Lena made a show of looking at her watch but she had twenty minutes free until her next class.

"You got the survey about bullying?"

"She's already done!" Sharon exclaimed, picking up the paper to show Ryan.

"Wow!" Smiling, he locked eyes with Lena. "That's what I like to see! I knew you were the perfect person."

Oh, God.

When he realized she wouldn't respond, he said, "I was thinking it would be great if someone with a lot of experience was at the board meeting tomorrow night. We really need someone with historical perspective to be there if there are questions about what the school used to do about bullying. In the past."

Shifting her weight from foot to foot, Lena forced herself to make a small smile before answering, "I was at last month's board meeting. It was my turn in the rotation."

"Oh, Noreen is going to be there tomorrow. I don't want you to take her place. It's just, she doesn't have a lot of experience on this issue and your input would be invaluable."

"Well, thank you. And, per your comments on the survey, *all* teacher input is invaluable."

Ryan laughed, rubbing one of his palms on the front of his khakis. "Okay, you got me there. But your input, it's really, uh . . ."

"Old?"

He glanced at Sharon. "This is why I like Lena. She's got a sense of humor. Actually, I was going to say *appreciated*. Your input is so appreciated because you have such historical perspective."

The phone rang. Sharon picked it up and said, "Coventry Middle School." Covering the receiver, she whispered to Ryan, "It's Mrs. Cauder, Finn's mother."

Ryan pointed to his office and Sharon told the caller she was transferring her to the principal's line. He took a step and turned back to look at Lena, saying, "So, can I count on you?"

"I'll give it some thought."

His phone ringing, Ryan smiled fully as he reached for it. "That's what I like about you, Lena. You're a team player."

She thought of stopping in the teachers' lunchroom to share the latest with Jen, but she wouldn't be able to talk freely there. Too many ears. Walking back to her classroom, Lena studied the pattern on the linoleum floor, wondering whether to throw Ryan a bone and go to the meeting. Oh, the survey. Well, as soon as he reads it, he'll bar me from the meeting. She smiled, imagining Ryan approaching her and saying, "You know, I don't want Noreen to feel as if her input isn't enough. Let's keep it to just one teacher at this meeting." Well, she'd be lucky if it went that way instead of a meeting in his office to discuss what he probably deemed subversive behavior.

She sensed movement in the corridor and looked up to see Jessica Freedman at the other end. The girl should have been in the cafeteria having lunch with the other eighth graders. Jessica stopped outside of Jen's classroom and peered in.

Lena called, "Jessica!"

The girl turned her head to and away from Lena and then went in the classroom. Lena walked hurriedly down the hallway to the room and entered it. Her eyes traveled over the neat rows of desks that Jen promptly straightened after every class. There were orderly piles of paper on her desk and a cup of pencils already sharpened. Nothing seemed to have been touched, but where was Jessica? Lena raised her eyes to the back wall and scanned the lockers. The one on the end, next to the window, wasn't entirely shut, and now the door seemingly moved on its own. Lena thought to joke, say something like, "Come out, come out, wherever you are," as though it were a game but she paused. Jessica, so obnoxious with her phony compliments. Jessica, the bane of her existence during third period. Lena had a wild impulse to walk to the locker and press it shut all the way.

"Hello, Mrs. Meyers!" Jen entered the room. "Word in the lunchroom is you're the first to turn the survey in. You get the gold star." Jen was carrying a steaming cup of coffee, blowing on it, as she walked to her desk.

"Oh, boy," Lena laughed, "just wait till he reads what I wrote. You didn't tell anyone?"

"Nope. I just said, 'That Lena. She's such a go-getter.'" Jen pumped her fist in mock triumph.

"That's me. Morning go okay?"

"I think so. I wasn't awake enough to notice otherwise. How about you?"

Looking at the locker, Lena spoke more loudly. "Oh, yeah, the usual. Jessica Freedman likes my sweater. She *really* likes it."

"Oh, her," Jen said. "Last week she *really* liked my earrings. She interrupted me at least half a dozen times to tell me."

Walking to a student desk, Lena sat down, her back to the lockers. "It's sad the way some students beg for attention. Jessica thinks she's being so clever but she's so obvious." Lena crossed her legs and glanced over her shoulder. "I may have to call her parents."

Jen opened a drawer and took out a package of gum, offering Lena a piece. "She's in foster care."

"What!" She waved off the gum.

Nodding, Jen said, "Yeah, she's been in and out of foster care. I guess there was abuse in the home. Her mother's boyfriend is in jail, so, put two and two together."

"Oh, my God."

"Yeah. Rough." Jen left her desk and opened a window. "Hot flash. I shouldn't be drinking this hot coffee. Yeah, so I cut Jessica some slack. She's been through a lot."

Lena stood. "Say, do you have a minute? There's something I want to show you in my room."

"Sure."

The women walked across the hall, Lena searching her mind for something to show Jen when they got there. It would only take a minute for Jessica to get out of the locker, leave the room, and get down the corridor. As they stepped into her classroom, the school phone on her desk began to ring. Will. He had tried her cell and when he didn't get her, called the school. She picked it up and said, "Will?"

"No, it's Sharon. Ryan wants to talk to you. Could you come to the office?"

Lena rolled her eyes at Jen. "Actually, I need to get some work ready for my next class. Could you tell Ryan I'll come down after next period?"

"Okay." The secretary sounded uncertain.

Hanging up the phone, Lena laughed and said, "Well, I think he's read my survey!"

"You're getting called on the carpet!"

"Yup, I'm in for it now."

"What are you going to say to him?"

"I guess I'm just going to have to feign innocence. 'Oh, did my survey upset you? I was just trying to offer helpful advice.'"

Jen clutched her stomach, laughing. "You're so convincing! I could almost believe you. I wish I could be there when you tell him."

"You can come with me."

"Oh, no. You're on your own!"

"Okay. I'm going to call Will and let him know I'm in hot water. He always gets a kick out of these things."

"Tell him hi for me. I'm going to run to the ladies' room. Oh, what did you bring me in here for?"

"It can wait."

As Jen turned to leave, Lena poked the numbers on her phone and again heard the recording of Will's voice. He sounded so calm, so friendly. She heard the alarm in her own voice as she said, "Honey, *please*, I'm getting worried. Call me or text me as *soon* as you get this. Please." She set her phone on her desk and stared at its blank screen. If she stared at it long enough, maybe it would ring.

From the hallway, she heard Ryan's voice call, "Jen! Just the person I'm looking for. Have you seen Lena?"

Not now. God, not now. Lena felt her forehead split with sweat. She looked at the space beneath her desk, wondering if she could crouch there but the thought of Ryan finding her cowering there flashed through her mind. Stifling a laugh, she slipped out of her shoes and ran softly to the back of the room, stepping into the last locker by the windows. She crouched against the back of it and used her index and middle fingers to close the door as completely as she could without latching it. She took a slow, deep breath and held it. Through the three slats at the top of the lockers, she saw Ryan enter the room, Jen behind him, looking about nervously.

"Oh, she's not here," Ryan said. "That's odd because she told Sharon she was getting ready for class." Ryan stood still, his hands on his hips.

"Maybe she's in the ladies' room," Jen said.

"Oh, well. Tell her I need to see her as soon as possible."

As he strode out, Jen behind him, Lena's cell phone began to ring. *Will!* She wanted to leap out of the locker, run to the phone, but what if Ryan returned and saw her jumping out of the locker like an insane person?

The walls of the locker pressed against her shoulders. The dark was disorienting but the stillness, the dead quiet unnerved her more. She told herself to breathe but there was no air in this metal box. *Jessica, I'm sorry.*

Pushing the door, she stepped out, miscalculating the distance to the floor, and stumbled, her hands breaking her fall. She grasped a chair affixed to a desk and stood, trying to fill her lungs although it seemed as if only a trickle of air was entering her. But she had to move, she had to expend the energy that was coursing through her.

She walked to her desk and picked up her phone, her fingers suddenly too big to easily locate recent calls. With her pinky, she navigated the buttons until she heard Will's voice, so relaxed as he said, "Sorry, I worried you, Honey. I had the nicest morning listening to Copeland. It just seemed like the perfect day to listen to *Appalachian Spring*. I couldn't get enough of it. I listened to it over and over. The beauty of it!" Lena heard him chuckling on the tape and then he continued, "It's embarrassing but I started crying. I just felt so euphoric, I had to. What's more wonderful than music? Well, you, of course." Then the long beep signaling the end of the tape.

Her breathing slowed and deepened. She heard conversational sounds growing louder in the corridor as the students, back from lunch, filled it. She heard laughter, shouting, the pounding feet of someone who was running down the hallway. Lena looked back at the lockers and knew she'd stay after school today. That she'd fill every garbage can in the school with all those books and journals. Her lockers would be completely empty before they took them away to stand in a new place.

YOGA FOR YOU

Mother has always been incredibly flexible. The muscles in her calves and thighs are long and lean, and she moves with the supple grace of a ballerina. There's not an extra ounce of flesh on her lovely, sculpted arms, raised now over her head as my sister and I pull her wedding gown into place, smoothing it over her narrow hips and adjusting the peasant ruffle at the top. It fits her as well as it did when she first wore it forty-four years ago. Sylvie has brought a picture of our parents on their wedding day and thinks we should get a picture of them today, the day of their vows renewal, holding this photo. I don't argue with Sylvie, but I'm going to need some serious liquor to get through this.

We fasten the loops of pearls she's wearing and brush her shoulder-length gray hair. Sylvie insists that she wear it exactly as she did the first time she and Dad married although I think it would be lovely in a chignon at the base of her neck. Mother was something of a hippie back in the day, but she has an elegant self-assuredness now that will undoubtedly elude me always.

The minister is already here, the small cake and champagne are assembled on a table in the enclosed courtyard of this nursing home, and the photographer should arrive at any moment. Dad is in his room, unaware that his daughters are readying his wife in a room down the hall, although he hopefully remembers that today is the big day. Sylvie had the florist make a bouquet of tiny pink tea roses with a ring of baby's breath encircling them, the final nod to authenticating Mother's original wedding day ensemble.

"Isn't it so sweet, Kit?" she asks me, her voice pleading with me to share her excitement.

"So sweet," I echo as I offer a silent prayer: Please, Dad, recognize Mother today. Pull it together.

❦   ❦   ❦

Mother's lithe and strong body is the fruit of her yoga labor. She's been at it for some forty years. When other mothers on the block started walking and jogging to lose the baby weight, Mom was doing downward dog on our front lawn, almost scandalous in suburban Ramsbury. She learned the basic moves watching that lady in a leotard on television who, after each pose, would say, "Bounce it out. Bounce it out," as her knees went up and down on the mat. Mother was younger than the woman on television, but she wore old sweatpants instead of a leotard. Sylvie and I wore our matching bathing suits as we tried to copy Mother's positions. I was a year older but people mistook us for twins all the time. We weren't as flexible as Mother, but we found the yoga poses hilarious. Happy Baby always made Sylvie fart, and we tumbled over each other laughing. "Good thing she can't hear you!" I'd shout, pointing at the lady on the television, and Sylvie took that as a challenge, determined to expel more gas as she rolled on the floor. At dinner, we'd show Dad basic moves. "This is Royal Pigeon," I told him, my legs folded beneath me so my hips felt a tremendous tug. Dad looked at me, bemused, and said, "I only represent the common pigeon. It's the royal ones who shit on my car."

They'd met in law school, our parents, married right after they graduated, but mother never practiced. She got pregnant immediately with me, was sick throughout the pregnancy, delivered me, and was absolutely delighted to do it all again a year later with Sylvie. She never seemed to care that she didn't practice law. She said that she and Dad always wanted a "house full of babies," but none came after Sylvie. Mother went to the doctor but refused to get the shots he recommended to stimulate her ovaries. Then she read an article about inner peace increasing fertility and threw herself headlong into transcendental meditation. "It's good enough for The Beatles, Paul," she told Dad who wiggled his eyebrows at me and Sylvie and said, "From now on, I only answer to Ringo."

"Dad!"

Sylvie and I danced through childhood like woodland sprites, laughing, always laughing, because we knew we were adored. Dad adored Mother, she adored him, and they both adored us. Couples on the block started to divorce, our friends going here and there for weekends and holidays. Sylvie and I were always at home and every kid in the neighborhood was welcome. Greta Henshaw, whose mother had coped with divorce by becoming a compulsive shopper and hoarder, was at our house so much that we thought of her as an honorary sister. And the other kids on the block were over regularly. Mother made us all cinnamon toast and squirted us with the hose on hot days. She organized games of kickball on our front lawn and joined in when we played hide and seek. She only took a break to watch yoga on television.

When Sylvie was in first grade, Mom went to what she called "Yoga University" and became a certified instructor. Then when the neighborhood kids came over, she had all of us in the backyard inhaling and exhaling and getting on all fours to do Cat and Cow. "You're warriors!" she called out to us as we positioned our legs in a lunge and raised our arms. We were her first class.

When I was ten, Mother opened her own studio, Yoga For You, in a reconverted store near the town pool. Sylvie and I went to the studio after school each day and did our homework. There weren't many people in the first classes but her reputation grew and before long every mother in Ramsbury wanted to sign up. Mother herself was the best advertisement for the studio, fit and beautiful. At some point, she had to put a cap on the number of people in each class because of fire laws. Dad wanted her to open a bigger studio or charge more for her classes, but Mother was happy the way things were. She added one class, then another, and soon was teaching around the clock. If she was flexible before, now she was a rubber band. There were pictures of her on the studio walls doing the Rooster, the Peacock, the Super Soldier. Her students studied the photos, trying to put their heads down while a thigh went up, or hold a plank for more than a second. They'd collapse, defeated and exasperated, only to study the photos once more and try again.

For me and Sylvie, the woman in the photos was our mother. We recognized her smile even though her head was upside down and her hair was piled on the floor beneath her. That woman with the leg wrapped around her neck? "Our mother made of rubber." Sylvie and I described her that way to everyone. Nothing could break someone made of rubber. Dad was so proud when she got an award from our local Chamber of Commerce. It hung in the studio next to a photo of Mother in the Embryo pose.

The first hint of trouble with Dad happened when I was in eighth grade. One night when he and Mother were talking late in the kitchen, I crept down the stairs and heard the word, "embezzlement." I didn't know what it meant but since Dad was crying and saying, "I'm sorry, I'm so sorry," over and over to Mother, I knew it wasn't good. Dad was going to be allowed to resign "in lieu of charges being pressed." He had to repay the money. I heard Mother's voice, soft, reassuring, telling him they could take out another mortgage on the house or sell the yoga studio. "No, Molly, not the studio," Dad said. "I'll eat crow in public before I let you sell the studio."

It was strange having Dad home during the day as he tried to launch a private practice. Sylvie still went to the studio after school but Mom suggested that I "be there for Dad" and go directly home. What did that mean? There were times when he sat on the couch and stared out the window for an hour at a time. I was supposed to do something, I realized, but what? I learned to make coffee and brought him a cup whenever he got too quiet. When Mother got home, she'd try to get him to do left nostril breathing, but he'd balk and say, "You know I think that's all nonsense!" But Mother was determined. She sat in front of him and made him copy her breathing. Sometimes dinner was late or we'd just send out for pizza because Mother wouldn't leave Dad, telling him to inhale to a count of four, hold his breath for a count of seven, and then exhale to a count of eight, over and over. "Good, very good," she said softly. "You're doing great."

And then it seemed as if Dad really was doing great. He rented office space in town and got some wealthy clients. He hired a secretary and a junior partner. His client list grew, his mood improved, we moved into a bigger house, and he had an affair with a woman named Thea.

Looking back, it was clear that the reason his mood improved was the affair with Thea or, maybe, just the sex. Dad was in his early forties then, ripe, I guess, for a mid-life crisis. I had no sympathy because I was having a crisis of my own. I'd found Sylvie crying under the covers of her bed more than once. One of her classmates had told her that Dad belonged in jail, that he'd gotten away with a crime. Leaks like that are like mice, there's never just one, and Sylvie feared all her classmates were talking behind her back. That was bad enough, but she said to me, "What's happened to Dad? Who is he?" When a fresh wave of tears broke onto her freckled cheeks, I resolved to never tell her about the affair. There was no guarantee she wouldn't find out, though. Thea seemed rather stupid, calling the house at all hours, Dad walking with the receiver on a long cord into the bathroom and talking softly.

Did Mother know? She wasn't around a lot then, flourishing in her own success. Or maybe she did know and that's why she was never home. Sylvie and I worked in the yoga office after school and it was there that Mother hugged us tightly and asked us about our day and told us over and over that she loved us. We worked in the office until we went away to different colleges, Sylvie finishing high school a year early because, I suspected, she could no longer handle being at home.

❀   ❀   ❀

I've often wondered if Sylvie was trying to recreate the early years of our life. She married Greg, her boyfriend of two years, right after college, taught third grade for a year, and had her first baby. A German major, I went to Vienna for grad school, fell in love with the city and stayed to teach college after I finished my dissertation. I was always mailing gifts home for Sylvie's expanding brood. Mom's letters were full of news of her grandchildren and my refrigerator was decorated with their pictures, my favorite one a shot with Dad wearing a miniature cowboy hat, the newest baby in his arms and the older kids hanging off his shoulders.

I had just been named chair of my department when Mother phoned and told me that Dad had returned one day to his first office, all of his former colleagues retired, and told a woman to take dictation. Mom retired from teaching yoga to stay home with Dad and sold the yoga studio for a healthy profit. She often asked me if I needed money and mailed me checks even though I assured her I was fine.

At the start of this summer, Dad wandered off a few times when Mother was in the shower and one day became belligerent when she found him in a neighbor's yard. He refused to return home and she had to call the police. It took three officers to restrain Dad, one of them retreating to the squad car when Dad gave him a couple of good kicks to the shins. The next time he wandered off, the police told Mother she needed to "make other arrange-ments."

Other arrangements. Of course I was concerned about Dad but I was more worried for Mother. What a mess to fall in her lap. When I expressed concern on the phone, though, she said, "Kit, yoga is the template for my life. Dad and I, our marriage, well, it's simply moved into a different phase, a difference pose, that's all. Dad and I will get through this."

And, in a way, they are getting through it. Mom's yoga money is now paying for a private room and care from a well-trained staff at Doniger Home. "His sense of humor is intact," Mom tells me as I pin a tiny cameo with a blue background to the front of her dress. "He has the housekeepers laughing from dawn till dusk with stories of his clients." During the last year, Mother had often remarked to me on the phone about Dad's "playful" humor. Shaking her head, she continues, "If some of them had any idea how many people know their business. Mrs. Creighton and her disinherited sons!" When she laughs, she sounds girlish, and I'm immediately taken back to the days of cinnamon toast.

When Sylvie first phoned me in Vienna to tell me of Mother and Dad renewing their vows, I'd asked, "Whose idea is this?" There must've been something accusing in my voice because she'd lowered her own and said, "Well, mine." She rallied though with "But Mother thinks it's a good idea." When I didn't answer, she said, "Kit, who knows how long Dad has left. He and Mother have been so devoted to each other all these years. This will be endearing, a bookend for the end of their lives together."

Sylvie, still such a romantic as she heads to middle age. I told her, "Mom says there are days Dad doesn't know her. He sometimes thinks she's one of the employees. And he gets agitated around a lot of people. Who are you planning to invite?"

Quickly, she answered, "It'll just be you and me and Lacey and Jason." They're her two younger children. She added, "Dan can't get away from college."

"Greg?"

"He's out of town that week on business."

"Oh, well, don't you want to schedule it for when your husband's back?"

"No! Their anniversary is May fourth. It *has* to be that day."

That meant I had to arrange for one of my teaching assistants to take my classes for several days. I'd be gone at least a week. I asked, "Will Dad even know he's at a wedding?"

Across the wire came crackling sobs and then her halting words. "Do you remember? When we were little? And Mother and Dad used to talk about their wedding day? Dad always saying that Mother was prettier than any woman on the cover of *Bride Magazine*?"

I did, and maybe that was why I closed my eyes and gripped the edge of the table. There were memories so dear, they were just unbearable. Unbearable because they didn't last. Nothing does. I tried not to think of those early days too often but Sylvie held them as closely as her own shadow. She said, "Wouldn't it be something if Dad looked at Mother in her wedding dress . . . and remembered? If even just for a minute, or even the *merest second*, he looked at her and remembered their wedding day? How wonderful that would be for him, and for Mother." Her breath poured out of her in a convincing gust that swept across the Atlantic Ocean and into my ear in Vienna.

So, I agreed to go to the wedding because clearly my sister was not going to be able to recover if her dream didn't come true. And, being the realist in the family, I knew it never would. I had to be there to pick up the pieces.

🪷   🪷   🪷

I flew home two days before the big day and ran errands with Sylvie, visited with my niece and nephew, in their late teens and great company, and accompanied Mother to Doniger Home to visit Dad.

Seeing him there was disorienting and difficult. He didn't recognize me although Mother insisted that he did, that he'd just forgotten my name. I didn't think the staff were as amused by him as Mother reported. More like shocked. When he told an aide that the steak on his plate was shaped like Lake Michigan and he couldn't eat it because he was afraid of drowning, she did laugh, thinking, of course, that he was joking. But then he threw his silverware on the floor and pointed at her, shouting, "This one's trying to drown me!"

The woman who took his laundry hamper each Tuesday was "that thief." Dad tried to wear all of his boxer shorts at the same time, one over the other, for safekeeping "Dad," I said, exasperated, "she only wants to wash your underwear. She's not stealing it."

He looked me over, head to foot, and said, "What do you know about boxers?"

He had me there. I'd had only a few boyfriends and I ended the relationships when they started to get too serious. My current boyfriend, Rolfe, was going to be old news very soon. I knew I wouldn't ever be happily married. Even if Dad hadn't had an affair and gone a bit bonkers before he really went bonkers, it ended like this. One of the spouses having dementia, the other standing on her head to make him happy. It wasn't for me. I knew I could never be like Mother, calmly pulling out a new package of underwear from her tote bag and handing it to Dad. He studied it carefully while Mother quietly put his laundry hamper out in the hallway for the aide.

When she returned, he'd given Mother a questioning glance and said, "Hey, lady, how'd you know my size?" Mother laughed, as if he'd told a joke, but I could tell Dad was suspicious of this woman who knew the girth of his hips and more.

In the car on the way home, I asked her, "Are you bringing him new underwear every week? That's insane."

Her smile was sad but her voice calm and even when she said, "Oh, Kit, why not spend a few dollars if it helps keep Dad calm. He'd do it for me if the situation was reversed."

I don't think so.

The ceremony can't be just immediate family and the minister because the nursing home stipulates that a staff member be present. Sylvie is going over last minute details with me in the borrowed room while Mother, feeling thirsty, is off in search of bottled water. My sister is wearing a sly smile as she discusses the required staff member. "You're not going to believe who works here."

"Who?"

"You'll see. She's with Dad now."

"*Who?*"

"I want you to be surprised. Oh, and Dad can't see Mother before the ceremony. I told her to wait in the visitors' lounge after she gets her water till I come for her."

"You've got to be kidding. We're doing *that*, too?"

Sylvie is crestfallen. "It's *tradition*."

Reaching my hand across the table to touch hers, I say, "Okay. Anything for tradition. I'll bring Dad into the courtyard and wait with him while you escort Mother in."

Sylvie nods. "That's just what I was thinking. I'm kind of the maid of honor and you're the best man."

"Oh, thanks a lot."

Winking, she says, "Well, you're taller than I am. Okay, I'll bring Mother in at two on the dot. We've only got fifteen minutes so I'm going to go meet her." She raises her arms and slightly shakes her fists. "Aren't you excited?"

"And then some."

Walking into Dad's room, I see he is dressed in a jacket and tie, his damp hair freshly combed. His glasses are slipping down his nose, but there's no denying he's still a handsome guy.

"Dad, you look great! Who helped you?"

"Me," a cheerful voice answers.

I turn around and see Greta Henshaw, our honorary sister from the old days, in a corner of the room. She's wearing an aide's uniform, a pin with her name on it on the smock. She's chubby and pretty and I lose it. I start crying and clasp her to me. "I can't believe it!"

Greta laughs and squeezes me back. "I know! I was updating the roster of patients on this floor one day and, lo and behold, I see Paul Kinsella! I came right to his room and we had a nice visit."

I wonder, did they really? But Dad is beaming. He seems happy, as calm with Greta as he is with Mother.

"Dad, do you remember Greta from the neighborhood?"

He frowns at me. "Of course I do! She was always watching cartoons with you and the other one."

"Sylvie."

"That's what I said!" He points his finger in front of him and moves it to the right as he continues, "There was you, Sylvie, and this one, always sitting on the couch watching those cartoons."

He remembers that? There's a catch in my throat as I gesture to Greta and say, "Greta. Her name is Greta, Dad."

His eyes grow large behind his glasses and he says loudly, "I know that! Didn't I just say that?"

Greta lays her hand softly on Dad's shoulder. "Kit has been in Europe a long time. She forgets what we know and don't know sometimes." She gives me a wink.

Pushing his glasses up his nose, Dad says, "Yeah, this is the one who went to Vienna. I told you about her."

"You did," Greta says in a voice that is calming and praising at once. Like Mother, she has the most soothing voice.

"Greta, bring me up to date? You're living here in Ramsbury?"

"About twenty minutes away. But my husband works here, so we drive in together."

"Nice!"

When I don't ask, she says, "And we have twin boys, fourteen."

"Oh! How wonderful!" I always forget to ask about kids.

"Your Mother told me about your job in Vienna. It sounds so glamorous."

"Well," I laughed, "I don't know about that, but I really like my job. If you're ever in Vienna . . .

We both laugh and she says, "The farthest I get these days is the Walgreens in Littlefield."

Glancing at the clock on the wall, Greta says, "Okay, Mr. Kinsella, it's just about time to go to the courtyard. Remember what we talked about. You were married once, a long time ago, and today you're renewing your vows to your beautiful wife, Molly."

"I always say to her, 'Good golly, Miss Molly!'"

Sylvie should be here to hear these words we heard throughout our childhood. It would make her so happy. For the first time since I've been home, I think this wedding may actually happen.

"Would you like to take my arm?" Greta asks Dad. I think that should be my job, as best man, but Dad stands so quickly and slips his arm through Greta's like they've been practicing. Grateful, I follow her and Dad out of the room and down the hall.

Sylvie and Mother are standing side by side in the courtyard, the minister a few feet away. Lacey and Jason are seated in folding chairs. The photographer, holding a hefty, complicated-looking camera, approaches Dad and Greta and the camera flashes, the light scorching my eyes for a moment.

"Oh, don't photo me," Greta says, covering her eyes. "I'm no one important." But the camera flashes again, brighter this time, and I can barely see.

I expect Dad to yell at him but he just blinks over and over, moving his head left and right, up and down, as Greta continues to walk him to Mother.

Mother. She is stunning, standing so erect, her posture so perfect, holding her bouquet and smiling with bright, wet eyes. Greta slips her arm out of his and goes to take a seat.

Dad calls out, "Hey! Where you going?"

"Just over here," Greta replies in that same soothing voice.

Sylvie and I also take seats. She looks at me, tears running down both sides of her face, and I rest my arm on her back.

The minister, a short, paunchy man with a gray ponytail smiles and says, "Well, we're all here. Shall we begin? We're here to witness the renewal of wedding vows between Paul and Molly."

"Molly? Who's Molly?" Dad's voice bellows and Mother says simply, "I am, Sweetheart. I'm Molly."

But he knew her name in the room. What's wrong? I notice he's still blinking and wonder if the flash of the camera has thrown him.

Dad looks at her, lifting his glasses off his nose and bringing them down again. "Well, I'm Paul."

"Yes, Sweetheart, you're Paul. I'm Molly and you're Paul and we're renewing our wedding vows."

"Wedding vows?"

The minister looks uncomfortable. I don't know how much Sylvie told him about Dad. Is there some minister code of ethics about not marrying people who are incapacitated in some way? Drunk or stoned or not of sound mind?

"Dad," Sylvie stands and steps forward, "We talked about this. You and Mother were married forty-four years ago. See, she's wearing the very same dress. And we thought it would be nice if you and Mother got married again."

Dad looks at the minister and says, "He's not one of the doctors?"

Now the minister bites his lip, probably trying not to laugh, and shakes his head. "No, Paul, I'm not a doctor. I'm an ordained minister. I'm here to officiate the ceremony."

Mother has never stopped smiling. She reaches and holds a side of Dad's face. "Darling, I'd like to marry you again. It's been forty-four years and I'm so grateful."

Dad sticks a hand in one of the pockets on his slacks and, jiggling the fabric, says, "Well, if I'm going to get married again, I'm going to do it right this time." He points at Greta. "I want to marry that one."

Sylvie gasps and I'm shocked to find myself already on my feet, running up to Dad, whispering, "No, you can't marry Greta, Dad! You're already married. To Mother. To Molly."

He looks at Mother, then back at Greta. He does this several times and I think I'm seeing a glimmer of understanding in his eyes. His eyes lock with Mother's and she says, "Paul, would you like to renew our vows?"

He says nothing. Mother strokes the side of his face and says, "Paul, it's our forty-fourth anniversary. We were married forty-four years ago today. Our girls, Sylvie and Kit, have arranged this ceremony for us."

As Mother speaks, I nod, Sylvie nods, Greta, from her seat, nods. Dad stares at Mother, then asks, "Can I have those flowers?"

Smiling, Mother hands them to him. "Of course you can."

Then, with the biggest grin possible, Dad turns and walks to Greta, hands her the bouquet, tries to kneel, almost manages, and says, "Will you marry me?"

Then everyone is talking at once. Me, Greta, the minister, and, loudest of all, Sylvie. Towering over him because he can't stand without help, my little sister looks down at Dad and yells, "*What the fuck is wrong with you!*"

"Oh, Sylvie, no," Mother says, moving adroitly on her heels to her daughter. "Don't say that."

If it weren't for Mother's pained expression, I think I'd be cheering Sylvie on. Where did she get the gumption?

"Where would you be without Mother?" my sister continues, punching the air around her with her fists. "Who else would have put up with your crap *all these years?* I'll tell you: *no one!*"

Greta and Mother, working together, manage to get Dad to his feet and then settle him in a chair. "Perhaps this isn't the best time for this conversation," Greta says.

Mother, her arm now around Sylvie's shoulder nods. "She's right, honey. Let's go somewhere and talk."

"Are you pleased with yourself, Dad?" Sylvie seethes. "You ruined what was supposed to be a beautiful day. You've always been so selfish, so weak, such an incompetent fool . . ."

"Okay, we're done. We're done." Mother takes Sylvie by the hand and leads her out as if she's a disruptive toddler. I notice the incredulous looks on Lacey's and Jason's faces. Perhaps I should stay with them, but I can't. I have to go with my mother and my sister. Almost out of the courtyard, I hear Dad say to the photographer, "Hey, take a picture of me and this one."

We go to Dad's room where Sylvie picks up a coffee mug, raises it in the air, but doesn't throw it. "I'm so fucking mad!"

I hug her and say, "I'm with you."

Mother takes the mug and sets it on the nightstand.

"Girls, take a deep breath, a slow deep breath."

"Mother, you've got to be kidding! You can be angry," Sylvie says. "For once in your life, let yourself be as angry as you want!"

I sit on Dad's bed and realize there's a bad odor, probably urine. "Sylvie's right, Mother. You can't make an excuse for Dad today. I was ready for him not recognizing you, maybe backing out of the ceremony, but proposing to Greta? Too much!"

Mother lowers herself gracefully onto the bed, beside me. Motioning to Sylvie to sit next to her, the three of us sit there in silence for several moments, Mother's arms moving in small circular motions on our backs. Finally, she says, "Dad has been taking care of me almost since I met him. It's my turn."

Sylvie rolls her eyes at me. "Please, Mother. You're scaring me. I'm worried you're as loopy as Dad. It's *always* been you taking care of Dad."

"No, not true." She shakes her head. "Perhaps I should have told both of you everything."

"Mother," I say, "We were there. We saw it all."

"Yeah, Mother. We both know about Dad stealing the money from the firm."

Mother's gaze is as stern as I've ever seen it. Again she shakes her head. "You didn't know I almost lost the studio early on and Dad took the money to make sure I didn't. And he always intended to pay it back. It was wrong but he did that for me. He did everything for me."

My sister and I look at each other, questioning looks. I'm wondering if Sylvie knows more about the family drama than I do and I know she's wondering the same about me.

"What else?" Sylvie leans against Mother and that causes Mother to lean against me. "What else did Dad do for you?"

Mother sighs. "I never wanted you girls to know, but I had a nervous breakdown in law school. I had to be hospitalized." She says this simply, as if she's saying she burned dinner. Mother's the calmest person I've ever met. She's the last person in the world who'd have a breakdown.

Both Sylvie and I lift our heads off her shoulders to look at her.

Nodding, Mother says, "Girls, I would never have gotten through that without your father. He was with me every step of the way. He proposed to me while I was in that hospital. I thought I was going crazy and would never be able to function in the world, but . . . well, his proposing gave me faith in myself. I got out, finished the third year of law school, and married the man of my dreams."

My sister and I, our mouths hanging in the exact fashion. People might still mistake us for twins.

"Is that why you never practiced law?" I asked. "Because of the breakdown?"

Mother makes a tight smile, then nods.

"No!" Sylvie says. "You wanted a house full of babies. You always said that."

"Oh, absolutely! You girls, my girls," she says, dropping a kiss on each of our heads, "you brought all the joy, all the happiness. Why, holding each of you as newborns, I couldn't imagine being depressed ever again. You saved me. First Dad did, then the two of you did."

I reach and trace the face on Mother's cameo. "And were you always happy?"

Mother seems surprised I asked. Her eyebrows lift as she says, "Pretty much. Oh, in the early years, I was scared my demons would come back. I'll admit it. The idea of the two of you having to come visit me in a mental hospital, well, that's really why I started meditation, then yoga."

"I thought you did meditation to get pregnant," Sylvie says.

Glancing up at the ceiling, Mother closes her eyes and then opens them. "My girls, so smart. I could never get anything past you two. Well, I was worried that if I couldn't get pregnant again, that I'd go down the rabbit hole again. I so loved being a mother. You know, there's nothing like being needed and being able to satisfy a need. It gives you purpose, helping someone. And newborns need help round the clock. There's no time to think about anything else. And when you love the person, well, that just makes it all the more rewarding."

Mother, I think, isn't really talking about her daughters right now; she's talking about Dad. In an odd way, maybe he is helping her. God knows he needs help around the clock. Sylvie is scratching her chin and I can tell she wants to say something, but she stays quiet.

Everything is out on the table. Well, not everything. I almost don't ask, but if I don't now, I never will. For years, I've felt guilty that I kept a terrible secret from Mother. She's told us her secret and I need to tell mine. In one word. I look Mother in the eyes and ask, "Thea?"

Sylvie inhales loudly and I understand that she knew. All those years ago, she knew.

"Yes, Thea," Mother says matter-of-factly. "She was my therapist when I was in the hospital. She'd retired by the time Dad had his difficulty with the firm. Even if she hadn't, Dad would never have agreed to go see her, but I did convince him to have phone sessions."

Together, Sylvie and I repeat, "Phone sessions?"

"Yes. Why? What did you think?"

I try to shake my head imperceptibly at Sylvie. After wanting everything out in the open, I don't want Mother to know that her daughters thought their father was having an affair. It would only make her feel bad, bad that we thought that of Dad and bad that we suffered. There had been enough revealing of family secrets today. Sylvie and I would talk it through, later. I sense a shift in our family, though, as a result of all Mother has told us. Now, it won't just be Mother taking care of Dad. Sylvie and I will help, too. Dad has enough needs for the whole family. Standing in this miserable, smelly room, I'm surprised that the idea of leaving Europe is, well, not terrible.

I stand. "Should we go find Dad?"

Mother smiles at me. She looks at Sylvie and taps her on the nose. "No yelling, okay?"

Sylvie looks sheepish. "I'm sorry."

"Don't be." Mother cups Sylvie's face with her hands. "You planned a beautiful day. I'm so grateful." She looks up at me and smiles. "And you came all the way from Vienna to be here." She stands and holds me. "It's been such a gift, having you here." She pulls Sylvie off the bed and into our embrace. "Having both of you here with me, I'm so happy. I want you to know that I'm so very happy."

The three of us stand together, our arms interlocked, the sides of our faces touching. It's a circular pose. We sway ever so slightly, our breathing becoming synchronized, in and out, in and out.

EVERGREEN FARM

Miriam was not upset when her son, Ben, married Carla, an energetic young woman with glossy black hair trailing over her hips. Her daughter-in-law taught kindergarten and her voice always bore the mixture of patience and exuberance one used when speaking to children. It sometimes annoyed Miriam, but she saw that her son construed it as attentiveness, and perhaps it was. Ben was Miriam's only child, she had tried to have more but couldn't, and given what she had endured in her teens, it was miraculous she'd been able to conceive and give birth at all. Since her husband's death three years ago, Ben was her only family in the United States. Miriam, Ben, and Carla celebrated the holidays and high holy days together. They went to the synagogue on Rosh Hashanah and Yom Kippur, and celebrated Thanksgiving, Hanukkah, and Christmas in each other's homes.

Carla was eager to embrace any Jewish tradition or custom, and talked of their children, when they had them, growing up fully knowledgeable of both Judaism and Christianity. Miriam couldn't fault her. She admitted to herself that it would have been nicer if some of the holidays could have been celebrated more quietly, as she and Ben used to celebrate them before his marriage, not with Carla singing full force over the Menorah. But still, the girl was trying; she was to be commended. So when Carla phoned Miriam one Saturday morning in mid-December and invited her to accompany her and Ben for a drive out to the country to get a Christmas tree, Miriam felt she couldn't refuse.

"Wear boots," Carla told her, "the fields will be muddy."

As she prepared for the outing, Miriam put on her black gloves with the long, sock-like tops that covered her arms mid-way to her elbows. The fabric caught on the side of her index finger and she realized the finger felt tender. She removed the glove to examine it and found a hangnail. Bringing the finger to her mouth, she tried to bite it off but the tiny wedge of nail slipped between her teeth. From her coat pocket, she pulled a small manicure kit stored in a black leather pouch that zippered on three sides. Miriam tried to steady the scissors around the hangnail, but her hands were shaky and her vision blurred. As of late, she'd noticed that she could no longer read the numbers tattooed on her arm without her reading glasses. Well, that was one good thing about declining vision. She attempted to snip the irritating sliver of nail but jabbed her skin. The blood, a festive red, bubbled for a moment before it ran down her fingers. She went into the bathroom and ran cold water over the puncture until the bleeding stopped. Returning the scissors to the kit, Miriam decided to wait until the hangnail was a little longer before trying again.

❦   ❦   ❦

The ride out to the country took almost an hour. Miriam sat in the back seat of the couple's new Saturn and wondered how they would ever fit a Christmas tree into this compact car. She imagined the tree occupying the empty seat next to her like a passenger on the ride home. Ben drove, occasionally picking up a yellow piece of paper on which were jotted directions. He worked as a pharmaceutical salesman and was used to reading directions and driving at the same time. Carla, seated in the passenger's seat, kept turning around to make conversation with Miriam.

"When I was a little girl, we always went and chopped down our own tree."

Miriam had heard many stories about Carla's childhood in the country. Carla seemed to have found it very quaint, although she seemed equally pleased with her present life in Shaker Heights.

"We used to go to Mr. Burdette's farm right after the first snowfall and claim which tree we wanted," Carla said. "We'd go back a few weeks later with a saw and Daddy would cut it down."

Ben interjected, straining to look at Miriam in the rear view mirror, "The place we're going is supposed to be one of the nicest tree farms, Mom."

"Wonderful." Miriam hoped she appeared interested. She added, "Thank you for including me," and Carla flashed her ever-ready smile.

Ben made more turns and the plots of brown, naked land became larger and, Miriam thought, increasingly desolate. Patches of absent life. She was struck by the quiet of the country; it seemed ominous somehow despite her daughter-in-law's continuous chatter. Carla turned around and offered gum, but Miriam declined. She should know better, Miriam thought, than to offer gum to a woman with dentures.

They saw a huge green sign of an elf sitting on a Christmas tree, the words, "Evergreen Farm" painted in white with little red holly berries splayed throughout the letters. Ben turned into a small parking lot filled with gravel. They got out, Carla offering her hand to help Miriam climb from the back seat.

The first thing Carla noticed was the smell. Not the fresh, piney smell of evergreens which she had been expecting, but that foul, rural smell, dirt and manure rolled together into such an evil concoction she thought she'd gag. She looked around and noticed the cows across the street gathered in a clump at the wire fence, their eyes enormous and hungry. From behind a barn next to the cows came the sound of dogs barking excitedly. Two men in dark blue coveralls came towards the car. They were talking loudly, their voices hurling out over the open fields. The men were identical in their work outfits and red baseball caps with the letters, "EF" embroidered in splashy green thread. One of the men was very tall, well over six feet, and the other was noticeably short, bearing an uncanny resemblance to the elf on the sign, Miriam thought.

"Here for a tree?" one of them called, and Ben yelled back, his voice booming, "Sure are!" Since he'd married Carla, Miriam was continually surprised with how animated Ben had become. He had been so quiet growing up. Their house had been quiet, too, a middle-aged house even when she and her husband were young and first married. They'd met in a resettlement camp in Poland, so grateful to fall in love, to come to America together and stay with a distant cousin of hers until they found their footing. They didn't expect or need anything else. When Ben was born, even their joy was quiet, almost fearful. Happiness was so new and therefore so fragile.

Miriam's husband had worked nights as a security guard for a bank for years before going to college in his early thirties. When he was a guard, he slept during the day, Miriam and Ben speaking softly to one another so not to disturb his rest. Only at dinner did they raise their voices to normal volume.

Ben was four the day a siren blared through the neighborhood, startling Miriam as she was pouring hot water into her tea cup. She'd acted instinctively, setting the kettle back on the stove, running to pick up Ben from the carpet where he'd been playing with a puzzle, and shutting both of them in the closet beneath the stairs. She didn't realize she was sobbing until Ben asked, "Mama, why? Why are you crying?"

She hadn't wanted to frighten him. She only wanted him to feel safe, safe and loved. That's all she ever wanted. Poor Aaron, her husband, asleep in their bedroom. After she settled Ben, she would have to run to their room and rush him into the closet. She should make this seem like a game, not scare Ben. *It's hide and seek!* she could say but he kept asking her about her tears. She had to stop crying but the tears were coming from an island of terror deep inside, a terror that she'd never leave behind. She gripped Ben to her and he protested, "Mama, too tight. Don't hold me too tight."

The door unexpectedly opened and she saw Aaron, the understanding in his tired eyes. "Everything's okay," he said, trying to sound as nonchalant as he could. He leaned down to meet Ben's gaze and said, "How would you like to see a big firetruck down the street?" Ben clambered out of the closet and held his father's hand as they stepped out onto the porch.

For days afterward, Miriam watched Ben for a sign that she'd planted a seed of fear in him. Would he remember her crying in the closet every time he heard a siren? Aaron brought home a toy firetruck that Ben was so taken with, he slept with it. The truck could be made to release a siren with the push of a small button. Before pressing it over and over those first few days, Ben would say, "Don't be scared, Mama." She tried to smile and said, "Will you grow up to be a big, brave fireman?" but knew she and her husband would steer him to a safer profession.

Miriam watched now as her son stood next to these two men. The short one left to get them a saw, and the tall one accompanied them into the field which was divided into two parts. In the first, trees already cut lay rocking a bit in the chilly breeze. Miriam's eyes traveled over the fallen, triangle-shaped trees; they looked as if they were shivering on frozen dirt floor. The man explained that there were three different prices for these trees depending on their size, fullness, and whether they were a Scotch pine, a blue spruce, or a frasier.

The short man returned with the saw, a piece of jagged metal with a steel handle. To get to the back part of the field, where trees were still standing, they had to walk around a sagging fence of brown sticks. On the right side of the fence was a concrete platform elevated a few feet and about a hundred feet long. There were two red metal pieces of equipment side by side on the platform. One of them looked like a tiny cement mixer and the other consisted of a round metal stand beneath a latticed semi-circle of curved metal.

Curious, Miriam looked at them and wondered what purpose they could serve in such a place.

Ben accepted the saw from the man and the three of them headed out to the back field. They could see the trees in the distance, stationary, watchful, waiting in stiff lines for the inevitable approach of the next person with a saw. Miriam's heart rose and dropped. It is just a farm, only a farm, she told herself again and again. She forced herself to walk quickly to keep up with Carla and Ben.

"Let's split up," Carla said, "so we can cover the lot faster. If you see a really good tree, call out." Ben and Carla kissed each other on the mouth briefly before heading off in different directions, Carla already starting to sprint. Ben turned to Miriam and gave her an encouraging smile, nodding his head as if to say, *okay*? Miriam was disappointed. Of course she'd have preferred that Ben stay with her but she waved him off and set out on her own.

She walked slowly over the wet, muddy field. Dank water invaded her boots and soaked her socks, the comfortable web of cotton between the toes suddenly horrid, an enveloping cold and wet menace that worsened with each step. She looked at the ground cautiously, trying to avoid the worst puddles, but the sensation of sinking in the loose mud was equally threatening.

Everywhere she saw tiny, dark, circular stumps sticking up out of the ground, the only thing left of the felled trees. Miriam recoiled. The stumps looked like amputated limbs screaming for help, as if the rest of their bodies were buried beneath the earth. She looked up at the sky, eager to avert her gaze, and saw that it was a smoky, battlefield gray, the sun sadly missing as it usually was anywhere near Lake Erie in December.

She heard a rustling in front of her and her first instinct was to flee, but to where? Across the street to the cows? She saw Ben's face, his serious expression, and she relaxed. He doesn't like this place either, she thought, and she felt a surge of pride.

Ben came over to her and said quietly, "Carla's disappointed. Seems the good trees are gone and all that's left are these skeletons."

"Carla?" Miriam asked blankly, the satisfaction she felt just a moment ago leaking out of her.

Ben nodded as Miriam looked out over the field at the trees. Ben had come up with the right word: skeletons. These trees had large, gaping holes and bent frames. They looked crippled, deformed with starved branches bowing out to look pitiful. And many of them were so small, baby trees which looked as if they couldn't bear the weight of their own needles, let alone Christmas ornaments.

"Carla's gone to the other lot to see if any of the trees already cut look any good."

He took her arm, and Miriam stepped carefully, pointing out to Ben the jutting bark dotting the floor of the field. She expected that he too would find the sight disturbing, but he simply said, "Yeah, looks like most of the trees were already cut down."

They walked past the platform. Miriam guessed that it used to be a train platform, and entered the tinier front field. Anna could see Carla's red jacket hunched over the green bundles lying on the ground. She was feeling needles, turning the trees slightly to check for fullness. When she saw Ben and Miriam, she waved excitedly.

"Over here!"

When they reached Carla, she asked Ben to stand up a medium-sized Scotch pine. Ben looked skeptical and said, "I don't know, honey. Don't you think it's kind of a funny color?" he asked.

"What do you mean?"

Ben looked at it and cocked his head. His lower lip bunched against his upper one as he appraised the tree. "It's got a funny yellowish-green color, don't you think?"

Carla looked at it and said, "Yeah, maybe you're right." She turned around and said quickly, "What about this one? It's sort of bluey-green."

"Now *that* one I like," Ben pronounced. He walked past Carla and reached in his pocket for his gloves. Leaning over the tree, he put his hand through the needles until he reached the trunk. He hoisted it up, standing behind it, and asked, "What do you think of this one, ladies?"

Miriam was surprised that her opinion was being sought. She tilted her head, imitating Ben, and said, "Oh, I think it's very nice. Very nice."

Carla started at it silently for a few seconds and then said matter-of-factly as she flopped her arms up and down at her side, "Nope. It just doesn't do anything for me. No personality."

Ben laughed and released the tree. It fell forward in a swooshing thud, the very top of it grazing Miriam's boot. Ben and Carla walked over to the next row of cut trees, but Miriam stayed behind. She looked down at the tree and slid her foot carefully out from under it. Lying at her feet like that, she felt that the tree was pleading with her, but for what? To be taken home or to be left here in peace? Easing her body over the tree, she extended her hand, touching the needles, expecting to feel their tiny points press against her fingers. When several of the needles fell from the tree, spindly green teardrops in her glove, she brought her hand to her lips and gently pressed the needles to her mouth. She inhaled the verdant scent, a respite from the oppressive brown odor in the air. Rubbing her fingers together, she dropped the needles into her coat pocket.

Miriam walked away from the trees toward the train platform. She found the railroad ties beneath traces of soiled snow. The wood was splitting in places and the metal was rusted, powdery orange flakes everywhere. She wondered how long it had been since the tracks had been used, where they led, and what the trains had carried. Ben and Carla called to her and she lifted her head. She saw the couple standing at the edge of the field holding a rather tall tree between them.

"What do you think, Miriam?" Carla called.

She nodded her head. "Nice. That's the one."

The men attending the lot realized a purchase was near and walked to Carla and Ben. Both men grasped the tree's trunk and carried it horizontally to the platform. Miriam smiled as Ben and his wife came to her.

"Wait till you see this, Miriam," her daughter-in-law said. Carla held her mittened hands to her chin in anticipation. Ben put his arm around her and their bodies leaned into each other.

The men put the tree in the silo-like contraption, tying it in place with a coarse rope. The taller man pressed a lever and at once the tree began to jump in place with an electrocuting shiver, pieces of it, needles, flying out. Miriam stepped back and swallowed her breath in a gulp before shutting her eyes. Ben noticed and shouted to her over the sound which was like a dentist's drill, "It's to get all the loose needles off it." Miriam opened her eyes and looked at her son bending over to kiss Carla's forehead.

The tree continued to bounce and Ben began to imitate it, vibrating his body and making his voice come out in chopped, "*Uh-uh-uh-uh,*" sounds. Carla laughed, playfully hitting the front of his jacket with her mitten.

The man pressed the lever again and the tree stood motionless. Standing against the metal lattice, the tree didn't really look any different, and Miriam exhaled a long breath.

The short man undid the cord and lifted the tree towards the little cement mixer. He propped it into the wide end of the funnel while the other man pulled the base of the tree through the small end. He reached into his jacket and pulled out a ball of twine, nodding to the other man to turn the machine on. Instantly, the tree came spiraling through the small end while the man with the twine expertly bound it from the bottom to the top.

They stood the tree up and Miriam was astonished that it was now only a third the size it was before they had stuffed it through the machine. The tree's many little arms had been sewn up so tightly that it appeared more like a body than a tree, a body that was struggling against the twine to stretch, to breathe.

Ben paid the smaller man several bills and the man insisted on helping them carry the tree to the car. There was discussion as to the safest way to store the tree, but Ben finally put it in the open trunk, and the man fastened twine around the lid of the trunk and connected it to the tree.

"When Christmas is over," Miriam said to him, "do people bring the trees back so you can, what do you say?" she searched for the word. At moments, as she grew older, her English seemed to leave her and she struggled to find a comparable word in Polish.

"Recycle them?" the man said.

Miriam nodded. Recycle, she thought, trying to commit the word to memory. Like bicycle, she told herself.

"Some folks ask about that, but we don't do it. I tell them that where I live, about a half hour from here, there's a place where everyone brings them on New Year's Day and we have a big bonfire."

"Bonfire?" Miriam asked.

"Yeah, they set them on fire in this big field. It's wild. The trees go up in these huge flames, crackling and spitting like all get out. We all drink hot chocolate, or something stronger." He laughed and winked. "It's a lot of fun."

"Sounds like it, " Ben said.

For a moment, Miriam felt she might fall to the ground. Something between her temples seemed to be pushing her backwards and she feared she would lose her balance. She shut her eyes fiercely and counted to three. The sensation passed and she breathed deeply.

Ben listened attentively as Carla talked about how her family chopped up their Christmas trees and threw the branches one at a time into the fireplace. Ben's arm circled his wife's waist and he lifted her an inch or so from the ground. Miriam was often embarrassed by their open affection in public, looking away when they indulged themselves, but today she watched Ben carefully. He seemed so different, so unfamiliar, and she wanted to assure herself that he was still Ben, her Ben. His eyes shone with a wet, youthful light and his body seemed to spring with energy. Miriam looked at Carla, who was wearing a ridiculous pair of enormous white ear muffs, and felt a reluctant gratitude.

She waited until Ben and Carla rounded the car to open the doors before feeling in her pocket for the small manicure kit. Quickly she unzipped the case, glancing about to make sure that the small man had returned to the field to assist a family with two boys. Miriam was tiny, easily hidden by the raised trunk lid. She surveyed the twine and was careful to cut it in several different places. It only took a few moments, but she trembled. Slipping the manicure kit back into her pocket, Miriam walked around the car and smiled graciously as she slid into the back seat.

On the ride home, Ben and Carla talked about getting the Christmas ornaments down, stringing cranberries and maybe popcorn as well. Carla had a recipe for eggnog that called for cinnamon instead of nutmeg. Miriam listened to them, watching with grudging approval as Carla patted Ben's thigh and he, in return, squeezed her hand. This woman, this silly woman, made her son so happy.

Carla swung around in her seat, peeking around the headrest so Miriam could see her full face, and said in that indulgent, teacher's voice, "Miriam, you'll stay and have some eggnog with us, won't you?"

"Thank you, I would love to," Miriam said, smiling fully at her daughter-in-law.

Carla leaned her body forward into the back seat, her arm extended to reach Miriam's and said, "I'm so glad you came with us today."

Miriam didn't respond, but she put her hand over Carla's and held it there for several seconds. Ben hit a pothole and they all jumped in the air, landing with such a thump they exclaimed over it for at least a full minute. Carla was concerned about the tree, angling her body to peer back at the raised lid of the trunk, but Ben assured her that he had tied it snugly. Miriam removed her glove and looked at the tender finger she had injured earlier. She put it in her mouth, using her tongue to target the hangnail, and then deftly slid it between her incisors. She ground her teeth and pulled her hand away from her mouth, happy to feel that unwelcome bit of nail pulled from her skin. She tasted a strengthening bit of iron in her finger's blood before she slid her glove over her hand and clasped her hands on her lap.

MY NAME IS YOUR NAME

She thinks of that article her son brought her to read. It said that if you can't remember something, think of things you associate with it. For instance, if you can't remember the name of an actress, think about what movies she was in and who her co-stars were. Our memories live in neighborhoods, the article concluded. "Oh, I don't give a hoot about some actress!" she'd said, tossing the magazine on her bed. She wonders if her son remembers the neighborhood where he grew up, all those years ago when her husband was still alive. When she closes her eyes, she can sometimes see it. There were shrubs in front of the porch, she's almost certain. Shrubs that grew so high that they blocked the house. A boy in the neighborhood climbed up one of the shrubs all the way up to the sky where he encountered a giant. She shakes her head. No, that's just a fairytale. That's not real.

Her name is Eleanor. Or Elizabeth. Think! she orders herself, but she still can't determine if she's Eleanor or her sister is. Her sister. She should call her sister. But, no, her sister died. A few years ago. No more than ten. Does it say Eleanor or Elizabeth on her gravestone? She needs to check the name engraved on it and then she will know what her own name is. She could ask her son what her first name is but he is so exasperated whenever she asks him a question. Or his eyes start to mist the way they did when he was a child and struggled with his reading. She'd made little signs and hung them all over their home, word labels for bed, table, chair, window, room, on and on. She'd sat with him for hours and hours, making up little stories about words so he could remember them. When he arrived home from school each day, she'd say, "Yellow, Charles" instead of "Hello, Charles." And he learned to respond, "Y-E-L-L-O-W, Mommy." She'd been relieved when math came easily to him.

Now she doesn't live in a neighborhood. She lives in a big house with too many people. Or she did until she left. The last thing she remembers about that place was that she was outside with some of the other people who lived there, all of them painting on big white poster boards propped on easels. She'd waited until the teacher, a young woman who smelled like orange peels, stopped beside her and said, "Oh, how nice." The picture was of a little blue house in a garden with pink flowers, the sun overhead partly hidden behind a fluffy cloud outlined in turquoise. "You have such a sense of color," the teacher told her. "Do you like pastels?" She'd answered, "I like all the colors." Heavens, she thought, the world would be such a dreary place if it were only black and white. Nodding, the teacher said, "You're absolutely right. All colors are beautiful," and moved on to the person next to her. She wished her son had heard the teacher say that: *You're absolutely right.* Then maybe he'd stop worrying about her. She'd wanted to sign the painting but she didn't know if she was Eleanor or Elizabeth. She lifted her brush and painted a blue "E" in the lower right corner. Then she set her brush down and got up. Looking over her shoulder, the teacher said, "We're not done yet. Class isn't dismissed."

"I have to go to the bathroom."

"Oh, okay. Then come right back."

Inside the big house, a man took her arm. "Aren't you supposed to be outside?

She looked at him, at his odd mustache that was thicker on one side and said, "I'm done with my painting. The teacher said I could come inside."

He started to say something and she interrupted, "The sun's too bright. I'm getting a migraine."

A woman approached them and said to the man, "You're supposed to start the Bingo game in the lounge. They're waiting."

"Be right there." He turned to her and said, "Okay, go to your room. But don't wake up Alice."

She almost spat at him. "I'm not going to wake up Alice! She's been asleep forever. She's probably dead." She headed down the long corridor hung with pictures of residents who had recently died and went right out the front door. She'd lied about the sun being too bright. If anything, it wasn't bright enough.

🪷   🪷   🪷

She has been gone at least two days, she thinks. And one night. She'd eaten the chocolate bar that was in the pocket of her skirt as soon as she left the big house. She'd slept inside a church, on a hard pew. She woke up when she heard singing, a coat that wasn't hers covering her. When the people lined up in the aisle, she did too. The man up front gave her a small, moist cracker. She asked him if she could have another one. His eyes grew large and he shook his head. A woman behind her slipped her hand through her arm and said, "Come with me, dear," but she pushed her away and said, "I don't have to go with you!" She walked out of the church and down a street with lots of cars going past.

She likes the hum of the cars' engines, the rushing sound of air as they pass her. I used to drive, she thinks. I drove Charles to school and I drove to the office. I typed every day. Sometimes I had to use carbon paper and it was so messy. She says, "Now is the time for all good men to come to the aid of the party." I could still type, she tells herself.

The street is wide and lined with stores. Maybe one sells coffee, she hopes. That was a nice thing about the big house; there was always coffee. Her son encouraged her to drink it. "It's supposed to be good for memory," he always said. Once she had snapped back, "Then you drink it!" Maybe more than once.

She walks inside a shop with a large window and says to a man seated in a black vinyl chair mounted on a strange silver pole, "I'd like coffee, please. Cream and one sugar."

He smiles at her and closes the newspaper he's been reading. "I'm sorry, Ma'am. I cut hair."

Her hands fly to her head. She feels her hair, sparse and coarse, and says, "Don't you dare touch my hair!"

"I won't. Don't worry, I won't." He slides off of the chair and stands. "Ma'am, is there someone I can call? Do you need a ride?"

"To where?"

"I don't know. To your house? Do you live near here?"

She shakes her head. "I used to live in a big house. There were too many people. I left." She looks through the window glass. "Is the cemetery near here?"

"Cemetery? No. Ma'am, where do you live?"

He's going to be trouble. She points through the glass door. "Over there. I'm going now." He opens the door for her, saying, "If I can help you with anything, please come back."

She is hungry, so hungry. She walks on until she sees the place with
a smiling hamburger on a big sign. She crosses the street and sits at a table
outside the restaurant. She sniffs. The scent of grease and salt is heavenly. She
is so hungry, she could die. She has no money. The big house people took her
money. Thieves. She knows if she demands food at this restaurant, they will
call someone from the big house. She puts her head on the table and starts to
cry. She realizes her underwear is becoming wet and thinks, I'm crying there,
too.

"Ma'am? Ma'am? Here, Ma'am." A man, chubby and short, puts a bag
in front of her. "You have to leave after you eat that. Okay?" Despite his size,
his teeth are large, his eyeteeth so pointy! The better to eat you with my dear,
she thinks, and is too frightened to say thank you before he walks away. She
unrolls the folded top of the bag and takes out a warm sandwich wrapped in
oily yellow paper and French fries in an open box as red as a fire truck. Next
to the bag, God bless him! the man had set a cup of coffee, packets of sugar
and a little capsule of cream, the seal already pulled back a bit for her. The
food is strange and delicious. A slimy pickle coated with too much mustard
sticks to the roof of her mouth. Pushing at it with her tongue, she swallows
and then coughs over and over. She waits until her throat finally relaxes,
takes a gulp of coffee, and wonders why the man didn't bring ketchup for
the French fries. At the big house, there is always ketchup in little bowls on
the table, no squeeze bottles. You have to use spoons to put the red sauce on
your food. Alice, stupid Alice, thought it was soup one day and ate an entire
bowl of it. The big house people then made Alice eat in the special dining
room, the small one where young women cut your food and feed it to you.
Chewing the last bite of her hamburger, she thinks, I don't ever want to eat
there with Alice.

❀   ❀   ❀

She walks and walks and hopes she's going in the right direction. The
shops are gone now. She sees houses with driveways, some with cars in them.
She comes to a patch of sidewalk with pictures drawn in chalk. On one seg-
ment, there is the smiling face of a little girl with squiggly yellow hair that
looks like the ramen noodles they sometimes have for lunch at the big house.
There are drawings on the sidewalk too, pictures of trees and a cat, or maybe
a dog, some four-legged creature with triangular ears. She walks up the driveway and sees that the drawings continue on a small concrete path next to the

garage. Rainbows, many of them, thick and thin arches of color that blend in places. She looks at each one of them, taking steps, and comes to the house's backyard.

Is this a backyard? She gasps and covers her mouth. There's another house here, a tiny pale blue house with white shutters around a little window, and a pink door. The roof is a real roof, lovely little slate shingles. She turns to look at the large house in front of the backyard and sees that the shingles match! There's a flower box under the window filled with daffodils. Daffodils! She hasn't seen them in so long. When she bends to inhale their scent, though, they smell like the shower curtain at the big house. She touches what appears to be a delicate blossom but it's firm between her thumb and finger. She turns the doorknob and stoops to enter the tiny house. Once inside, though, she can almost stand up straight. She has to crouch just a bit. She looks about, marveling at the little furniture. There's a wooden rectangular table with two chairs, all painted a soft pink. Puzzle pieces, mostly black, white, and red, are scattered on it. Studying them, she guesses that, if put together, the picture would be of a cow standing near a barn. There's also a somewhat larger rocking chair painted white although the paint is peeling on the arms. There are no lamps but there's plenty of sunshine coming through the window. The walls are made of particleboard and painted pale yellow. The floor, wide wooden slats, is stained a dark, dark brown. So practical, she thinks; it doesn't show the dirt.

She tries to sit on the rocking chair, grasping the arms and lowering herself. The seat is too narrow but, yes, there now, with her legs crossed, she can almost manage. She looks around. Isn't there supposed to be a chair that's too big and a chair that's too small and one just right? With her one foot on the floor, she pushes to make the chair rock and smiles as she closes her eyes. She marvels that her stomach is full and she has found a little house. So little the people in the big house will never find her. She is home.

She must've fallen asleep. When she opens her eyes, a small child is standing in front of her, a little girl with blue eyes and springy blonde curls. She remembers the chalk picture of the girl with ramen noodle hair. Smiling, she says to the child, "Why, hello. How are you?"

When the little girl smiles back and says, "Good," she sees that the child still has all of her baby teeth.

"Well, that's fine, dear. Tell me, what's your name?"

Stepping closer, the little girl puts her hands in the pockets of her dungarees and answers, "Lizzie."

She cups her cheeks with her hands. *Lizzie!*

The girl scratches her cheek and says, "What's your name?"

She leans forward, bringing her face close to the girl's and says, "Guess what? My name is your name."

The girl's eyes expand. "Really?"

Nodding, she blinks to keep tears from slipping down her cheeks. She doesn't want to frighten this little cherub. "Yes, I'm Lizzie, too. Why, when I was your age, my mother used to call me 'Busy Lizzie' because I did so many things. I took dance class and I took elocution lessons. Oh, they don't teach them any more, Sweetie, but they were lessons that taught you to speak well, to project your voice when you were doing a recitation. A recitation of a poem or a speech. Sometimes I'd forget the words. Oh, I would get so mad." Grinning, she clenches her hands and shakes them for effect. "Then my mother would say, 'Lizzie's in a tizzy,' and that made me even madder," she laughs.

Lifting her eyebrows, her chin coming forward, the girl says, "I know the ABCs and I can count to fifty."

"You can?" She opens her mouth widely and flops a hand to her chest.

Proud, the little girl nods and starts to count. When she finishes, the woman claps and says, "Well, *that* was a recitation! A very good one!"

Smiling, the girl says, "I know a lot more than Teddy."

"You have a Teddy bear? You know, I did, too. Actually, I had a whole collection but my favorite was Theodore. He was named for President Theodore Roosevelt."

The girl puts her hands on her hips, saying, "*No*, Teddy is my *brother*. He's two and a half."

"Oh! Thank you for explaining that. And how old are you, Lizzie? A big girl like you, you must be . . ." She lowers her eyebrows to appear to be thinking hard.

"Four!"

"Four! Why you are a big girl, aren't you?"

"Yes. Why are you here?"

She says nothing. Shifting in the chair, she realizes that her hip hurts, that it is pressed up against the arm of the rocker. Finally, she answers, "I came to meet you, Lizzie."

Whispering, the little girl says, "I'm not supposed to talk to strangers.

Don't tell Mommy."

She inhales and struggles to stand. "Well, Lizzie, we're not strangers any more and it was so nice to meet you." She stoops to shake the little girl's hand.

Lizzie says, hope in her voice. "I could tell Mommy you're not a stranger. If she knows we have the same name, maybe she won't think you're a stranger."

"Thank you, Lizzie, but your mommy is very wise. We shouldn't talk to strangers. I have to be on my way."

At the door, the woman turns to wave to the little girl. Lowering her head, she steps through the doorway and finds her way around the side of the garage and back onto the sidewalk in front of the house. Squinting in the bright sun, she looks left, then right, before remembering that there's no need to find the cemetery. She knows her name. Elizabeth. When she was little, everyone called her Lizzie. And then, in college, Liz. She has been Liz for so many years although her son calls her, "Mother." She would like to tell him about the tiny house and the girl, little Lizzie. He will be amazed that she has had such an adventure. But how will she find Charles? Oh dear, she thinks, I was supposed to leave a trail of breadcrumbs.

She hears a voice call, "There she is!" Turning, she sees Lizzie with a woman, a tall woman with squiggly hair like Lizzie's but darker, almost brown. The woman is holding a small boy wearing a blue hat that ties under his chin. She looks worried but then mothers often do. Still, the three of them standing there together make such a nice family. In this sunlight, she can see them so clearly.

ACKNOWLEDGEMENTS

Some of these stories were published, in slightly altered form, in the following publications:
"The Cigar Man" was published in *Soundings East*
"Reservoir" was published in *PMS* (poemmemoirstory)
"Marcasite" was published in *Temenos*
"Sisterly" was published in *Minerva Rising*

Many grateful acknowledgments to June Goodwin, Rob Hardy, Nina Jaffe, Judy Kuns, Megan Mitchell, and Barbara Savage Huff for reading and advising on some or all of the stories in this collection. Thanks and a heavy dose of maternal love to Madeline Geitz for assisting with manuscript preparation. For his fabulous instruction, encouragement, and enthusiasm throughout my writing career, I remain ever thankful to the late Joe David Bellamy. His own writing continues to offer guidance, inspiration, and joy. Finally, boundless thanks to Heather Tosteson and Charles Brockett for finding me and welcoming me into the Wising Up Press family where I've received unflagging support and a profound sense of literary community.

Kerry Langan is the author of two earlier books of short stories, *Only Beautiful & Other Stories* and *Live Your Life & Other Stories*. Her short fiction had appeared in more than forty literary journals published in the United States, Canada, and Asia, including *Other Voices, StoryQuarterly, American Literary Review, The Antigonish Review, Rosebud, Thema, The Seattle Review, The Cimarron Review, Fireweed,* and *Yuan Yang,* as well as in on-line journals. She was also a co-editor of the Wising Up anthologies *Shifting Balance Sheets: Women's Stories of Naturalized Citizenship & Cultural Attachment, Creativity & Constraint,* and *Siblings: Our First Macrocosm.*